Lainey's Lot

Lainey's Lot

Lisa Tenzin-Dolma

Published by Accent Press Ltd 2016

ISBN 9781786150172

Chapter One

Kieran

Love cracks you open like an egg. It leaves you sizzling in a pan, too stunned by the liberation from your shell to realise that you're about to be eaten up. Well, that's how I felt when I met Kieran Kamau. Crack. Sizzle. And then that wonderful and awful *ohmygod* moment when I knew that life would never be the same again. Quite how much my life (and his) would change was, fortunately, way beyond the scope of my imagination on that day.

I suppose you think I'm mad, talking about eggs. But, you see, it was eggs that started it. Half a dozen of them. Free-range, of course, because Mum won't buy battery- farmed ones. Anyway, there I was, humming my way along the road, (the song was 'One Summer Morning' by The Chickadees, in case you're interested) and I was counting the cracks in the pavement, as you do, when *splat!* I walked right into him and dropped the carrier bag.

The tomatoes rolled into the road to instant death by passing cars, the eggs broke, and I swore. Loudly. I can now testify that eggs will not fry on a hot pavement, but they did congeal a bit. I looked at the mess and knew, just knew, that Mum would slay me. Then I realised that the person, the bumpee, so to speak, was still there.

'I'm really sorry,' he said. Not, 'Why don't you look where you're going, you idiot?' which is what my immediate response would have been. I looked at him. He looked at me. Contrite brown eyes, like a puppy, and it took me a minute to notice the rest of him. It was worth losing the eggs for.

His skin was the colour of warm amber, the same colour as

the necklace that Aunt Bee gave me for my last birthday (my fourteenth, if you must know). She told me the beads had been formed forty million years ago, and I love that one piece has a strange kind of fly in it. Anyway. His hair was dark brown, almost black, and coiled in shiny ringlets all the way to his shoulders. He was wearing baggy jeans and a white short-sleeved T-shirt that made his skin look even more golden. And he was tall, almost a head taller than me, and I'm pretty tall for my age.

'Are you OK?' he asked, and I suddenly felt very, very stupid, staring at him, unable to say a word. I gave a squeak, and he bent down to pick up the egg carton and put it back in the plastic bag. It was full of bits of goo and eggshell, and I kind of knew how those eggs must feel.

Once he broke eye contact my voice came back. 'I'm fine. Sorry!' was the best I could say. I took the bag from him and ran, when really all I wanted to do was ask him who he was, where he lived, and whether he'd mind if I stalked him. I didn't look back.

Mum, as she tactfully put it, was Not Amused, and we had baked beans on toast for tea.

Chapter Two

Mum

My mum's a bit weird. She has idiosyncrasies, so I'd better warn you about them. For one thing, she collects words like other people collect CDs, or jewellery, or computer games. She's a word magpie. She reads through the dictionary as if it's an amazing cookbook or something, and chooses a word a day. I figure that she'll be about half-way through her collection by the time she's a hundred and five. One of the words, as you may have guessed, is idiosyncrasies, and when she's found the Word of the Day (WOD for short), she writes it on a post-it note, sticks it up somewhere around the house, then says it constantly all day. It's amazing how many sentences you can put together that include 'idiosyncrasy' or 'superfluous' or whatever the current WOD is, though sometimes she's hard-pressed to find something to say to Susie in the local shop that actually makes sense. And it can be horribly disconcerting to be innocently washing your face, then look up to find a post-it note on the bathroom mirror with 'Gargantuan' written on it. That gave me a complex for days, because I'd been trying to ignore the fact that I had a spot on my chin the size of Vesuvius, and I felt really self-conscious about it afterwards.

Mum's other idiosyncrasy is dancing. Now, I know dancing is fun. I like to do it, especially when Amy, my best friend, comes round and we have a makeover to the accompaniment of loud music. Most parents would yell, 'Turn that noise down!' Mum doesn't. Oh no, she comes jigging up the stairs and joins us! Mortifying. Amy, whose mum wears black suits to work and doesn't laugh much, says my mum is cool, but she doesn't have to live with her all the time.

Dancing in the house is bad enough, but Mum dances in the street too. If I'm unlucky enough to be out with her (I can be persuaded when she offers to buy me something to wear, for instance, which isn't often these days), she starts jiggling to the music that pours from every shop we pass. It can shift from Bob Marley, to Bolero, to the latest boy or girl band, and she just changes her movements to fit the rhythm as she trips along, which makes her look like one of those scary marionette puppet dolls. Sometimes she sings, too, sneaking in the WOD, and, believe me, it makes me cringe.

She's quite a good cook though, and she works part-time at a wholefood shop, so she gets given fresh foods that are near to their sell-by date. We've been vegetarian since long before I was born, and she's very strict about making sure I eat properly. No junk food, of course, which means that I sneak as much as I can of it at every party and sleepover I'm invited to.

But even in her cooking she has idiosyncrasies. She peels mushrooms, and won't eat the stalks (I like them raw, so do quite well out of her aversion). And (you won't believe this, but honestly, it's true), she takes the skins off chickpeas! It takes her ages, and she has A Method. She rinses the chickpeas, puts a bowl on her left, and has this nifty little knack of squeezing every single chickpea slightly between the first finger and thumb of her right hand, passing the now naked legume into her left, popping it into the bowl, and dropping the skin to her right. She says it's a meditative process and makes her feel calm.

Now you might have some idea of what I have to put up with.

But the day I bumped into Kieran (whose name I didn't know at the time, of course), and broke the eggs, and Mum was Not Amused, she decided to shell chickpeas for the next day, and that calmed her down. I sat at the kitchen table, watching, and asked her how old she was when she first fell in love.

'Thirteen,' she said. 'With Marc Bolan. But he died.'

'Oh Mum, that's terrible!' I was really shocked. 'Was he at school with you?'

Mum shelled another chickpea. She looked a bit sad, and I felt sooo sorry for her. I mean, what an awful thing to happen.

You'd be emotionally scarred for life.

'No, I never actually met him,' she told me. 'He was a rock star. Such lovely long hair. In fact, he'd been dead for a good few years when I first saw a video of him, and I cried for weeks after my mother told me.'

At that point I thought it might be a bit pointless to tell her about the gorgeous boy who had caused the egg-dropping incident. There's no way she would understand.

I swear I'm a changeling or something. I mean, I'm not a bit like her.

Chapter Three

Me

I know it's getting a bit late for introductions, but I was so carried away with excitement over meeting the Boy of My Dreams (BOMD for short) that I completely forgot to tell you who I am! My name is Lainey Morgan, and (as you already know, because I told you earlier), I'm fourteen. Actually, I'm fourteen and eight months, which really makes me closer to fifteen.

I live in Bath with my mum, and I quite like it here. In fact I like it even more now that I know the BOMD is somewhere close by – and is a real person, not like my mum's obsession with a long-haired, long-dead rock star. I won't tell you about school because that's too boring, but yes, I go to school (when I can't get away with pretending to have a sore throat or a headache). And I'm not the tallest girl in my class (that's Lucy Belling, and I swear she's going to be at least seven feet tall before she stops growing), but I'm the second tallest. In fact, at the moment I'm the second tallest in the whole school, though I'm hopeful that other people will have a growth spurt and catch up soon. Maybe it's all the chickpeas Mum feeds me.

I have long, straight, reddish-brown hair that I hate but my mum says is pretty, and very pale skin, so I get a lot of freckles in summer. My eyes are blue with little flecks of green in them. And I'm finally developing what Auntie Carol, who's a bit prim (perhaps she was a changeling too, or maybe my mum was) calls 'a figure'. I'm quite proud of that, especially as I was the last girl in the whole school to start sprouting, and I've become passionate about skinny crop tops, which Mum doesn't like buying me.

However, I'm quite clever in a non-academic way, (Mum's word would be 'resourceful'). I save up the bits of change that Mum lets me keep when I go shopping for her, and when I've got enough I trawl through the charity shops. There are loads of good ones in Bath, and I find skinny tops that fit, or are even a bit too tight, then cut the bottoms off them and make them look a bit ragged (not hard to do when you just grab one end and hack away with slightly blunt scissors). As Amy says, I make Fashion Statements, but she's a very kind person so she probably wouldn't tell me even if I looked stupid.

My idiosyncrasies are talking too much (especially now that I'm excited because I've met the BOMD), and having, just having, to make daisy chains when Amy and I go to the park. It's like a compulsion. I like draping them over Amy's hair, because she has curly, blonde hair that's quite long but not as long as mine (my hair reaches past my waist because my mum refuses to let me have it cut), and she looks like a princess, or a fairy, or that picture of Venus drifting around on a very large shell.

Another idiosyncrasy is caricatures. I'm very good at those, but it gets me in a lot of trouble at school. Mr Podd, the meanest, nastiest, most bad-tempered teacher I've ever had the misfortune to meet, caught me last week in the act of finishing off a brilliant caricature that I'd done of him when I should have been listening to the incomprehensible stuff he was spouting during History. I thought it was a good likeness, but he took dire offence at being portrayed as a slug, and I had detention for three days running after school, which was a far greater punishment than I deserved. Luckily Mum laughed when she read the letter of complaint that the school sent to her. She said that Mr Podd has no sense of humour, but that I mustn't do it again (or at least not in class). I had the last word though, because I drew it again when I got home, scanned it in, and emailed it to Amy, who emailed it to Hannah, who emailed it to Dianne, and so on. You get the drift, I'm sure. The next day, at school, the teachers kept finding copies of my work of art drifting around in the playground and tried to blame me, but as it wasn't the original I managed to get away with looking hurt and protesting my innocence.

As I said, I live with my mum. Not my dad. Before you get worried that Mum lost two of her great loves to the Grim Reaper (death, that is), they're divorced. My dad, you see, is a love rat, and Mum threw him out when she found him snogging some woman in a car outside the house. His excuse that she was just giving him a lift home from work, and had something in her eye, didn't wash with Mum, because their lips were glued together when she caught them. Gross.

Anyway, Dad is now married to the woman, whose name is Sandy, and they live with her four-year-old son by someone else, whose name is Ian (the son, I mean, not his father). Ian has behavioural problems or something, and takes up a lot of their time, so I hardly ever see Dad. Not that I want to, anyway. My mum might be weird, but we generally stick together, except when she's dancing.

We don't hear from Dad's family since the divorce. I don't think they ever liked Mum much, because Dad's parents, my paternal grandparents, used to make pointed remarks about how he should go home more often for a decent meal. As he ate at our house every day until Mum caught him devouring Sandy's face, I got the impression that 'home' meant their house, not ours.

My mum's parents, my grandparents, were carried away by the Grim Reaper when I was small (from the photos, he must have had a tough time lifting my grandma, because she was a very large lady, but I'm too polite to mention that to Mum). And my mum has two sisters and a brother.

Aunt Bee (the one who gave me the amber necklace), is a bit younger than Mum, and is funny and clever. She's an actress, but not a famous one, and she seems to get a lot of non-speaking parts in films where she pretends to be drowning, or gets stuck in lifts, so she doesn't usually look her best on the big screen. She goes out with a lot of actors, and says they're narcissistic but she can't resist them.

Aunt Carol is the oldest, and is married to Uncle Todd. She's very prim and proper, as I said, and never, ever swears, but she can be quite funny at family get-togethers because she has just one glass of wine and then talks a lot, saying 'Oops, naughty me!' when she says something even slightly rude.

Then there's Uncle Denny, who I adore, and who has a different girlfriend every time we see him. He's quite a bit younger than Mum. When I was little he used to tell me fairy tales. Not the ones in books, exactly, but he'd start off as if it was a story I already knew, and then ramble off in a completely new direction, so that the characters got lost in sewers and fought with giant rats and things like that. I used to love them (actually I still do), and was always begging for him to babysit me so that he'd tell me more stories. When Mum found out about the rats and so on, she told him he had to stop or I'd get nightmares, but it was stories like *The Little Match Girl* that used to upset me. I like rats.

Which reminds me. I have a white pet rat called Horace. He's really sweet and friendly, and his little pink nose twitches when he gets excited. He sleeps in a cage in my room, and Mum's quite strict about the cage since she found I'd been letting him sleep in my bed. It's a shame, because I used to like it when he curled up against my feet to fall asleep, but Mum said she couldn't afford to keep buying new sheets just because Horace liked to nibble holes in them. Horace sits on my shoulder while I do my homework and text my friends (I usually do both at the same time, which could account for all the school reports that say 'Lainey is not fulfilling her potential'), and he tickles my ear with his whiskers, and makes snuffling noises. It's a sort of rat whisper, and it makes me laugh.

Amy, as you know, is my best friend. I do have other friends (you'll meet them later), but she's the one I spend the most time with. She's quieter than me, which probably most people are, but Amy's the kind of quiet person who feels peaceful to be around. She's also smaller than me, but that's kind of obvious as I'm the second tallest girl around here and Lucy Belling's the tallest, so you might have already deduced that for yourself. (Deduced was Mum's WOD last Wednesday, and she began to sound like Sherlock Holmes after a while.) Amy's very clever. She's always top of the class in everything, and she wants to go to university and be a scientist when she's older, so I'll have to find a job in the same area so that we can carry out our grand plan of sharing a flat. With my grades, university seems a little unlikely, unless I find something that interests me enough to make me 'fulfil my potential'. I don't think you can get a degree in making daisy chains, though I'm hopeful that it might happen by the time I'm old enough.

As Amy's dad is not a love rat (and neither is her mum), she lives with both of them, two streets away from me. We met on our first day at infant school, and I was so enchanted by her hair that I couldn't resist pulling it. Fortunately for me, she only cried a bit and then agreed to be my best friend. And we've been best friends ever since. I told you she was kind. Amy's mum works in a bank, and her dad works in London, so he gets the train every day and comes home late. That means that Amy spends a lot of time at my house, so she doesn't mind. She sometimes calls my mum 'Mum' by mistake, and it makes me laugh and call her my sister. Mum says she's my honorary sister, and especially likes Amy because Amy never moans at her for dancing. Sometimes I think Mum likes Amy better than me because I get in trouble at school so much, but when I sulk about it Mum puts her hand on her heart and swears she loves me best. She says it was me that drove her to shelling chickpeas, though.

Chapter Four

Kieran

The next time I saw Kieran (you knew we'd bump into each other again, so to speak, didn't you, because I told you his name earlier) was in town after school on Tuesday. Amy and I were just coming out of the charity shop in Pulteney Street when I saw him across the road with Scotty Mayhew (AKA Spotty Mayhew, because he, erm, gets a lot of spots). Scotty is our mate Dianne's older brother.

I grabbed Amy's arm and hauled her back into the doorway, ignoring her squeak of surprise, and peeked out carefully.

'Ow, you pinched me,' Amy said, rubbing her arm.

'Sorry,' I hissed. 'That's him. The BOMD.'

We both peered out around the corner of the doorway, a bit like Horace does when I wake him up in the mornings. If I had whiskers they would have twitched. 'Look straight ahead, over the road, with Scotty.' The BOMD was wearing the same uniform as Scotty. Interesting. So he does live around here.

Amy stared. 'Ohmygod, he's gorgeous! So why are we hiding?'

'Because I'm having a BHD (Bad Hair Day), silly.' Mum had refused to let me straighten my hair, she said it was already straight and the heat would ruin it, so instead I'd plaited it the night before and now the top bits were crinkly but the ends were straight, and it looked a bit weird. I'd had this fantasy of looking perfect next time I saw the BOMD. No egg on my shoes, shiny hair like on a TV advert, nice clothes instead of boring school uniform, and he would swoon and dive into the nearest florist to buy me a dozen red roses. Mum's passion for romantic movies was starting to rub off on me.

'Lainey, your hair looks fine. Come on, stop skulking in doorways.' Amy stepped forward and gave my arm a tug. I tugged back, pulling her off balance.

'Let's go back in the shop for a minute,' I pleaded. Much as I wanted to meet him, a BHD wasn't going to make much of an impression.

Amy stepped out on the pavement, ignoring my urgent hisses to come back, just as Scotty and the BOMD started crossing the road. 'Scotty!' she called. They both looked our way. Amy waved. They headed towards us. I tried to hide behind the door.

'Hi Scotty,' said Amy. Scotty grunted. He's in the year above us, and it's not cool to be too friendly with your little sister's mates in front of other guys. However, I know for a fact that Scotty quite likes Amy, because he blushes when she's around. Amy says that he's always blushing, but I never see him do it at any other time, and she would say that, wouldn't she, because when she sees him she's *always there*! I carefully peeked out from behind the shop entrance. Sure enough, Scotty was looking a bit pink around the gills.

'Is Dianne in town?' Amy asked. I couldn't *believe* she was doing this to me! Sweet, kind Amy was luring them closer to the doorway!

Scotty shook his head. It was kind of funny that he found it as hard to talk to Amy as I did to the BOMD – who, at that moment, was looking casually in the shop window and happened to see me trying to hide behind the door frame.

'Oh, hello!' he said. 'We meet again.' I thought people only said that in films (maybe he likes romantic movies too!) and I was quite taken aback, not to mention utterly mortified at being caught out. But he had the most luscious smile, and very white teeth.

I mumbled, feeling my cheeks beginning to burn. 'I hope you didn't get into trouble after our accident,' he told me, sounding quite concerned. He had the loveliest eyes, and once I looked into them my head went all swimmy and I lost my voice. Again.

Scotty turned round. 'What accident?' he asked. Poor Scotty.

His cheeks were scarlet, like mine, and I got the impression that he was trying to keep us here so that he could muster up the courage to talk to Amy. Unfortunately for him, I knew that for months Amy has been harbouring squishy feelings for John Carter, who's in our year, doesn't have spots, and who has, so far, gone out with (and subsequently dumped) five girls in our year, and two in the year above. I get the impression that he's steadily chomping his way through the entire female population of Bath, and we'll have to start locking our mothers away from his ravening clutches soon.

Kieran winked at me. 'I bumped into her and she dropped her shopping,' he told Scotty, without taking his eyes off me. 'I'm Kieran,' he said, and looked at me questioningly. I still couldn't quite find my voice.

'Amy. And Lainey,' Amy said into the awkward silence, nodding in my direction.

'Lainey. Nice name.' All I could think was that I was stuck in the entrance of a charity shop, with the BOMD, on a spectacularly BHD. A woman with a shopping bag on wheels squeezed past us, tutting, and went into the shop. Kieran glanced at my hair. 'You look different today,' he said.

That did it. I grabbed Amy's arm, muttered, 'Gotta go,' and pulled her out of the doorway, heading up the road and round the corner by the weir at a fast trot.

'Why'd you do that?' Amy asked, trying to keep up with me and stay upright at the same time. 'He was nice.'

'BHD,' I muttered. 'Probably put him off for life. But if he hangs out with Scotty, maybe we can find out about him from Dianne.'

'Ah,' said Amy. She's great, despite the fact that she deliberately caught their attention when I least wanted him to see me. Amy never worries about BHDs, but she knows how sensitive I am about that sort of thing.

Chapter Five

Dianne

Amy, as you know, is my best friend. But Dianne hangs out with us quite a lot. Amy likes Dianne because she says she has a good sense of humour when you catch her on a cheerful day. Sometimes I'm not too sure why I like Dianne. She can make me laugh, but it can be hard to tell whether she's laughing *with* you or *at* you, and she can be very grumpy and snide at times. However, one of the reasons I like Dianne is because she's what Mum calls a maverick. She gets in trouble a lot, even more than me. Mum doesn't like Dianne because she says she's a 'bad influence', especially since we all went window-shopping and Dianne absent-mindedly put a Boots 17 lipstick (Cherry Red) in her pocket and we all got arrested just outside the main entrance.

Having someone around who's a 'bad influence' can be quite useful when you're considered to be a bad influence yourself, because it makes you seem much better behaved than you actually are. It takes the pressure off, so to speak. But the Lipstick Incident truly was due to a lapse of concentration. It's just unfortunate that Mum had to come and get us all from the police station, because Dianne's mum was out and doesn't have a mobile phone. Luckily, she just got told off very sternly, and wasn't sent to prison.

Dianne is the second oldest (Scotty's the oldest) in her family, and she has loads of younger sisters and a little brother. There's Adele, who's eleven, Sonia, who's ten, Jody, who's eight, and Jack, who's only five. Jack cries a lot, and his nose is always running. I find him very unappealing, and have decided that I'm never going to have children.

Their house is the same size as ours, so all the girls are squished together in one room, in bunk beds. Poor Spotty Scotty has to share a room with Snotty Jack, and their mum and dad have the other room. Dianne says she can't wait to leave home, because her sisters are always borrowing her clothes without asking (she would say no if they asked), and leaving them on the floor with chocolate stains all over them. And she says Adele snores, and Jody talks in her sleep. That could explain why Dianne always has dark circles under her eyes, but Amy, who of course is kind, helps her put concealer on when we go out together.

We went straight to Dianne's house, to find out as much as we could about Kieran. Dianne was pleased to see us, because it meant she could escape from The Hordes. Her mum gave us a packet of crisps and a drink each (Mum says their food bills must be horrendous), and we went to the park and sat where we had a good view of the boys who were skateboarding.

Now, Dianne is not always to be trusted. If you have a secret, don't ever tell it to her, because if she's in a bad mood she tends to hold it against you or, worse, to tell someone who doesn't like you. So tactics were called for in order to extract information. Amy kicked off, while I started on a daisy chain and tried to look uninterested.

'We saw Scotty in town,' she said casually.

'Oh,' said Dianne, not at all interested. Well, why would she be? She spends her life trying to get away from her siblings. Amy tried again.

'He was with someone called Kieran.'

'Mmmph,' said Dianne, putting three crisps in her mouth at once. I began to feel a bit frustrated, but separated the daisy chain in two, joined the ends, and draped one circlet over Amy's hair and the other over Dianne's hair.

'He seemed nice. Friendly.' Amy was careful not to look at Dianne. Instead, she adjusted her daisy crown and pretended to be very focused on a boy who was swinging back and forth so fast on the skate ramp that a fall was clearly inevitable.

'He's OK. Only moved here last month.' Dianne crunched the last crisp and screwed up the packet. 'Scotty's staying with him this weekend. They're going to youth club tonight. Lainey, can I sleep over at yours? If Adele doesn't stop snoring soon, I swear I'm going to throttle her.'

The boy fell off his skateboard, flipped it upright, and hobbled over to sit on the grass with a bunch of mates, trying not to look too bothered. Little cogs were clicking in my brain. I looked at Amy. She winked at me.

I tried to sound casual, even though my heart rate had increased considerably. 'OK. Amy's staying, but Mum won't mind if you do too. We were planning to go to youth club tonight.' Of course, we'd planned nothing of the kind, but how could I resist such an opportunity?

Amy covered her mouth with her hand so that she wouldn't laugh.

'It's boring,' Dianne groaned. 'Can't we watch a DVD instead?' Dianne was clearly not in a cooperative mood. I had a bright idea.

'We could give you a makeover. And you can borrow my green top if you like.' Now, if I say so myself, that was inspired! Dianne's eyes lit up and she leaped to her feet. She's coveted that top since Mum bought it for me last month. It's skinny and shiny, and has little pink beads in the shape of a heart on one shoulder. I had to do the washing-up for three days running *and* hoover once a day before Mum reluctantly agreed to buy it for me. As soon as I got the top, of course, the dishes piled up and moss started growing in the carpet, and Mum had to nag me again.

Dianne was suddenly very keen to go to my house and get ready. We rang her mum from my mobile phone (her mum sound pleased, relieved even, to agree), and hot-footed it arm in arm across the pavement to my house. Sometimes I'm a genius even though I'm not academic.

Mum, of course, was put on the spot when I asked if Dianne could stay the night. She gave me a dirty look, and was clearly not very happy about it. But I've discovered that, with Mum, when I ask favours in front of witnesses, she feels awkward about refusing in case she comes across as A Bad Mother. If it's just me, she usually says 'No.' So, despite the fact that she still hasn't forgiven Dianne for the lapse of concentration that culminated in our visit to the police station, she agreed.

You see? I may not be academic, but I'm not stupid.

Chapter Six

Youth Club

It took two hours to get ready to go out, because a great deal of preparation was necessary. Showers, hair-washing, (I'm not risking a Bad Hair Night as well as a BHD) and much discussion over what to wear. My entire wardrobe (such as it is – I don't have that many clothes) was spread out over the bed, and Dianne pounced on my green top while Amy and I tried on everything at least twice, in various combinations.

Finally Amy settled on her jeans and a blue top with floaty sleeves that I've had for ages and am bored with now, but it looks pretty and very fairylike on her. Dianne, of course, wore the green top with her own jeans. I settled on my red T-shirt with a jaggedy edge (I used pinking shears to trim it) and my short denim skirt with a flounce around the bottom. I'd read somewhere that red means passion as well as danger, and I hoped it would catch Kieran's eye and make him magically fall in love with me.

Then we did our make-up. Dianne has big eyes and looked tired, so Amy applied concealer and painted on eyeliner so that it flicked up at the edges. I put lots of sparkly eye-shadow on her, then Amy and I did each other's eyes and we all put on Amy's pale pink shimmer lip gloss. I closed the door and put a chair under the handle so that Mum couldn't barge in, and Dianne and I quickly straightened our hair with Amy's amazing straighteners that she'd sneaked into her overnight bag. Amy left hers curly, which looked great with the floaty top. Then we took the chair away.

Mum came upstairs just as we'd all sprayed on Black Orchid perfume, and said the house smelled like a bordello. (I had to look that WOD up later, and discovered that it means a house of ill-repute, so I hope she doesn't slip it into conversation with Susie at the shop!). We had the music on loud to get us into party mode, and Mum couldn't resist having a little dance. Amy laughed and joined in, but Dianne gave her a funny look and concentrated on trying to see her back view in the mirror. I really wish Mum would behave when my friends are here.

After Mum stopped dancing she told us that there was pizza and some salad waiting downstairs. I couldn't eat much, I was so excited. Then finally, *finally* we left the house. Dianne looked at her reflection in every window we walked past. She really likes my green top. I glanced in a few windows just to make sure my hair still looked OK. Amy, who's very modest, and who wasn't expecting John Carter to be there, didn't even bother to sneak a passing glance at herself. She really is cool, and I'm glad she's my best friend.

Youth club was quite crowded, because it was the once a month disco night and people from all the schools were there. I scanned the room carefully in case Kieran was already there, but he wasn't. So we sat in the corner with Hannah, Tina, and Rosa, whose parents are Italian and so she's stunningly beautiful. That worried me a bit in case Kieran liked her more than me – all the boys seem to gravitate towards Rosa, enchanted by her huge brown eyes and her tinkling laugh. I like her much better when there are only girls around. We danced a bit, and I kept going to the toilets to check that my hair looked OK and to put more of Amy's lip gloss on.

It was just starting to get boring when I saw Scotty and Kieran. Scotty was talking to someone from Year 10, and Kieran was standing quietly, listening. I nudged Amy. She looked up and followed my line of sight. Unfortunately, Dianne was moaning about how fed up she was with her sisters, and she noticed that I was suddenly distracted and looked over, too. Kieran must have felt our eyes boring into him because he half-turned, saw us, and waved. Amy waved back. I blushed. Dianne stared at me, hard, and started chanting. 'Lainey likes Kieran! Lainey likes Kieran!' Everyone nearby looked across at us and I dug her in the ribs.

'Stop it!' I hissed. 'I don't even know him!'

Just then Kieran and Scotty came over. Scotty, as usual, was very pink-cheeked. Kieran looked gorgeous in a black T-shirt and jeans. Scotty sat next to Amy, and Kieran stood quite close to my chair. Everyone stopped talking, and the silence felt very awkward. Dianne sniggered and I wanted to thump her.

'D'you want to dance?' Kieran asked. I looked around in case he meant Amy, but he was looking at me. I gulped.

'OK.'

He was a good dancer, and didn't embarrass me by jumping up and down on the spot or throwing his arms around like most of the boys I know. That impressed me even more. Then a slow tune came on, 'The Scent of Honey', about a man who's in love with a golden-haired girl. I turned to go back to the others but he touched my arm. 'Let's carry on dancing,' he said. Honestly, I thought I was going to faint when he swivelled me round and put his hands on my shoulders! I wasn't sure what to do with my own hands, so put them on his shoulders too, which was awkward because it meant our arms kept bumping together. He pulled me a bit closer and sniffed at my hair.

'You smell lovely,' he said. I swear, from now on I'm going to wear Black Orchid every single day.

The dance seemed to go on forever. I was torn between being really, really embarrassed and trying to take deep breaths so that I wouldn't faint from sheer delight. Neither of us spoke. The song came to an end and Kieran smiled at me, took my hand, and walked me back to my chair. His hand felt warm and smooth, and I was aware that mine was clammy with nerves. So humiliating!

Dianne was not looking happy. Amy was talking to Scotty about her aspirations to be a scientist, and Scotty looked as if all his birthdays had come at once. Poor boy, he still doesn't stand a chance against the temptations of John Carter's urban suaveness where Amy is concerned, but she's polite to everyone and doesn't seem to realise that he likes her. Kieran went and found a chair, and squeezed it in next to mine. Luckily he didn't mind talking, because I was still finding it hard to look at him and find something interesting to say at the same time.

He didn't even seem to notice Rosa, who dragged Dianne off to dance – maybe because she was annoyed at being ignored. It was a relief to escape from Dianne's Killer Glare for a few minutes, but I knew, just knew, that she'd give me a hard time later on.

So in the space of ten minutes I'd discovered that Kieran moved to Bath a month ago, that his dad's West Indian and his mum is French, but he grew up in London. His mum used to be a model and now runs a PR agency, and his dad is a writer. His life sounds very glamorous compared to mine. And Kieran sings and plays guitar in a rock band, and they played some gigs at his last school! He said he's going to be famous, and I believe him. He has star quality. Then he asked me about myself. I couldn't tell him that I wasn't 'fulfilling my potential', and that my only talents are making daisy chains and drawing caricatures, or that my dad's a love rat and my mum is a word magpie. So I told him about Aunt Bee being an actress (I didn't say that all the roles are small, or that she looks half-drowned in a lot of them), and that I liked swimming.

Bad move! He invited me to go swimming at the leisure centre on Sunday, and I suddenly realised that it would mean he would see me in my *horrible* school swimsuit, because my nice one was too small. I started to shake my head, but he put his hand on my arm and said, 'Oh, come on, Lainey. It'll be fun.' I took a deep breath and agreed.

Even Dianne's sniping on the way home couldn't knock me off the fluffy pink cloud I was floating on. Amy had told her about the eggs, and she kept saying things like 'Eggsactly,' and 'Eggscruciating' all the way to the house. I didn't care. I was too busy thinking, 'I'm in love.'

Chapter Seven

Very Bad News

The first inkling that something was very wrong came the next day. I had detention after school (again) for talking in class (well, it wasn't my fault that Hannah asked me who the gorgeous boy was that I was dancing with!), *and* for forgetting to do my Geography homework (I had more important things on my mind). So I'd texted Mum to say I'd be late home, pretending I was going to Amy's straight from school so that she wouldn't moan at me, and when I strolled through the door it was immediately apparent that Things Didn't Look Good.

For one thing, no cooking smells were in evidence, and there was a post-it note on the banisters with 'Censorious' written on it that made me wonder whether Mum had found out about Kieran and me holding hands. The other clue was that Mum and Aunt Bee were sitting together at the dining table with an almost empty bottle of red wine (and it was only seven o'clock; how decadent!), and a huge pile of bits of paper and brown envelopes scattered all over the table. Mum's eyes were puffy and red, and Aunt Bee was gesticulating wildly (she's so dramatic!) and talking very loudly. I just caught, 'This is a state of emergency, Ellen,' when they saw me come in and Aunt Bee stopped talking. Mum gave me a lop-sided smile, and I had a sinking feeling that this wasn't the time to ask whether she would buy me a new swimsuit for Sunday. It seemed more sensible to seem to be helpful and cooperative, in the hope of reciprocation later on.

'Sorry I'm late. Would anyone like a sandwich?' I asked, as if I hadn't noticed that the atmosphere was very gloomy. They both shook their heads, and Aunt Bee poured the last of the wine into their glasses and picked up one of the bits of paper. I went and made a cheese and cucumber sandwich, and took it upstairs to my room so that I could text Amy and report on the unlikelihood of getting a new swimsuit. She has three bikinis, so I thought I could ask to borrow one for the day, even though it might be a bit tight on me.

When I went downstairs for a drink later on Aunt Bee had gone and Mum was sitting in the dark, watching the real-effect gas fire flickering. I switched the light on.

'Are you OK?' I asked, even though I didn't really want to know. If Mum had problems she should talk to the grownups about it, not me. She's supposed to protect me from the harsh realities of the world. But it seemed weirder not to say anything.

Mum looked up, blinking a bit in the light. 'Sit down for a minute, Lainey,' she said. 'We need to talk.'

Oh, oh, I thought. That sounds ominous. I perched on the edge of the sofa, ready to leap up and leave the room if things got too heavy. Mum sighed and rubbed at her eyes.

'Your father's supposed to pay maintenance for you,' Mum muttered, 'but he hasn't been for quite a while, and things have been … well … difficult lately. I have a lot of bills to pay, and the only option to get things straight seems to be to sell the house.'

I was astounded. And horrified. 'You mean we have to move?' I asked. 'But I like it here!' My next thought was, I've only just met the BOMD, but I pressed my lips together tightly so that the words wouldn't come out.

You can imagine the rest of the conversation. Me pleading. Mum shaking her head and looking helpless. Me angry, then furious – with Dad for being an inconsiderate love rat, and with Mum for letting things get this bad. Mum told me that we'd have to move away from Bath. I said that I'd run away from home, or move in with Amy, or even (sheer desperation, this) with Dianne and The Hordes rather than leave here. Mum cried. I raged and cried at the same time. Mum tried to put her arms around me. I pushed her away and ran up to my room, slamming the door so hard that the pictures on my wall went all wonky.

The next day I played hooky from school, and went and hid in the park for the day. I knew the school would phone Mum when I didn't turn up, but I didn't care. Let her think I'd run away. It would serve her right. I texted Amy and asked her to meet me by what we call the Carved Tree Trunk, and told her the whole sorry story when she arrived. Amy was as shocked as me but, being kind, insisted on coming home with me so that Mum would know I was safe. She promised to lend me her nicest bikini on Sunday, even though really there's not much point in seeing Kieran if I'm going to have to move away.

Mum was very, very Upset and Worried. She phoned the police and Amy's parents as soon as we got home, and told them I was back, then said that maybe there was another option and we could rent out the house instead of selling it. But we would still have to move away. She gave Amy a big hug for bringing me home. I wouldn't let her hug me, and as soon as Amy had left I went to my room and refused to come out.

Chapter Eight

Dad

I thought very hard all night long, and made a decision. The next day I turned up at school for registration, then played hooky again and went to the insurance company where Dad worked. It's very posh there, and everyone seems to talk on the phone at once. How any of them can hear themselves think is beyond my understanding.

The receptionist wouldn't let me in because I don't have a work pass or identification, and she offered to phone Dad's office, but I wanted to catch him unawares so I told her not to bother, and left. Or rather, I *pretended* to leave, but waited outside the door until someone went in and started talking to the receptionist, then quickly sneaked past while her back was turned, and leaped into the lift before she saw me.

Dad's office is on the third floor, and he has a little cubicle in the corner of the huge room, because he's a manager. A few people gave me strange looks as I walked through the office, but most of them were talking too fast on the phone to even notice me. Dad was on the phone, too, and didn't even look up until I was standing right next to him. Boy, the expression on his face was soooo funny! He didn't look pleased to see me at all. I perched on the edge of his desk. 'We have to talk,' I said, copying the ominous tone that Mum had used with me. Dad looked around his office, mumbled 'I'll call you back', and put the phone down. Everyone carried on working.

'Not here, Lainey,' he said. 'Call me later on, after work.'

I raised my voice, so that everyone nearby looked up in surprise. 'We need to talk *now*!' I insisted. Dad looked worried, and shushed me. 'Mum says we have to move, just because

29

you're an irresponsible love rat and you haven't been paying maintenance,' I said, very loudly indeed. People started to whisper to each other. Dad jumped up and gripped my arm very tightly (it hurt), and steered me out of the office, down the corridor to the lift, and pushed me inside. I opened my mouth and *screamed*. Two men who were walking along the corridor stopped in their tracks and stared. Dad hesitated then stepped into the lift with me, and pressed the button to close the doors. The lift started going down.

'You've got to give Mum the money you owe her,' I said, almost in tears. 'I don't want to move.' Dad just glared at me as if I'd crawled out from under a prehistoric rock.

The lift reached the ground floor, and the doors started to open. Quickly Dad, grim-faced, pressed the button again and the doors closed. I caught a glimpse of people waiting outside, and they looked very surprised. The lift started going up again.

'I can't give your mother any money,' Dad said. 'Ian needs to go to a special school, and I can't afford to pay for you as well. She'll have to get a job.'

'She's got a job already,' I wailed. 'And she has me to look after. It shows how much you know about our lives. Ian isn't even yours!'

The lift doors opened at the top floor. More people were waiting outside, and they started to step forward. Dad, looking as if he might spontaneously combust, pushed the button quickly, and the doors closed in their faces. The lift went down.

At the ground floor, Dad let the doors open this time. Holding my arm tightly, with me struggling to get free, he marched me to the main entrance of the building and pushed me through the door. By then the receptionist had called a security guard, a huge muscle-bound man with no neck, and when Dad stalked back towards the lift the guard refused to let me back in. I sat on the steps for a while, trying not to cry, then went home. Mum was still at work, fortunately, so I made a cheese sandwich and ate it, then went back to school just in time for afternoon registration. I got detention for not doing my Maths homework, and a letter was sent to Mum about my misdemeanours. Sometimes life sucks.

Chapter Nine

Kieran

Amy rescued me from another row with Mum on Saturday night by inviting me to sleep over at her house. Her parents were watching a play at the Theatre Royal, so we spent the evening on our own, trying out her new light-reflecting make-up (her parents buy her a lot of goodies to compensate for not being on the scene much, and I can't help feeling a *teeny* bit envious sometimes). I tried on Amy's best bikini. It's a bit too tight around the chest, but Amy, being kind, said that it just made me look as if I have more cleavage, and that it quite suited me. I felt very sad about Mum insisting that we have to move, so we raided the fridge and found an open, almost-full bottle of white wine, and had a glass each. It tasted disgusting (like drinking vinegar), so we put lemonade in it and it wasn't too bad then, so we had another glass. Then we added water to the bottle so that Amy's parents wouldn't notice we'd had a little tipple.

But I discovered that it's not a good idea to drink wine when you're feeling upset. It just made me cry and cry, and I got streaks of make-up all over the white towels in the bathroom. Amy's cat, Mister Smith, came and sat on my lap on Amy's bed, and purred to make me feel better, and Amy gave me a can of cola (forbidden by my mum), and started to cry too, because she wants me to stay. All in all, the evening was a washout.

Kieran had arranged to meet me outside the leisure centre at eleven o'clock on Sunday. Amy walked into town with me (I was very nervous), and then went to see Hannah. I got as far as the entrance gates and nearly turned and ran home, but Kieran was already waiting, and he saw me and waved. I took a deep breath and waved back, but my feet suddenly refused to move me forward. I stood there, glued to the pavement, feeling very, very stupid. Kieran, looking perfectly relaxed, as though he wasn't nervous at all, strolled over and took my shoulder bag with the bikini and towels (and change of clothes, hairbrush, make-up, Black Orchid perfume, of course, shampoo, conditioner, and hairdryer – it was quite heavy) off me. I wasn't sure how close I should walk to him, so aimed for a nonchalant six inches between us, just enough range so that he could hold my hand if he wanted to. He didn't take my hand. He just chattered about how great Bath is, and how glad he is that they moved here.

Of course, that just made me want to cry again, because Mum was making us leave, and I'd only just met the BOMD, and all my friends were here. I tried to breathe deeply, and Kieran looked at me a bit oddly.

'Are you OK?' he asked.

I sniffed. Not a good way to impress the BOMD, is it? Especially on your first date. At least, I was assuming it was a date. Maybe he went around holding girls' hands at discos and inviting them swimming willy-nilly. I realised that I didn't know him at all, and I might be making assumptions, which made me feel even more depressed.

'I'm fine,' I told him, and we went up to the reception desk. Kieran insisted on paying for me, which led to a swift, embarrassed scuffle of protesting, getting out my purse and putting them away again. It did mean that he saw this as a date, I think, and it also meant I could now afford the skirt I'd had my eye on in the charity shop that just needed a few inches off the hem. Secretly I was delighted, and it cheered me up a lot. We separated outside the changing rooms.

Amy's bikini really was a bit too tight, but I figured that it would stretch in the water. I looked at myself in the mirror before going out to the pool, tried to ignore the bulges of flesh above the bikini top, and checked that the waterproof mascara was really waterproof by splashing my face. My eyelashes stayed black, so I ventured out, with the towel wrapped around my shoulders.

Kieran was in the water at the edge of the pool. He called to me, and I threw the towel over the pool barrier and very quickly jumped into the water. It was freezing! The pool's supposed to be heated, but it never seems very warm. Kieran splashed me, and I splashed him back, shivering, then we raced each other the full length of the pool and back and that warmed us up.

In case you're wondering: yes, he looked gorgeous. I couldn't get over how smooth and golden his skin was. And he's quite well built, with definition on his arms, and he was wearing boxer swimming trunks that made his legs look really long. Actually, they *are* really long. When we got out of the pool after an hour of splashing, racing, and ducking underneath the water to hide from each other, getting told off for bumping into people (the pool was crowded), we couldn't stop laughing, and I felt a lot more relaxed with him. We went and sat in the lovely warm Jacuzzi for a while, and closed our eyes while the water bubbled around us and my hair floated around getting whirled into tangles.

Kieran, I discovered, is very patient. He didn't complain about waiting over half an hour for me to get showered, dressed, do my make-up, and dry my hair. He just grinned and took my hand when I came out. Yes! He took my hand! We went to Bonghi Bo's cafe to sit outside and have a drink, and I told him about Mum's Big Decision. His face fell.

'But we've just started seeing each other,' he said.

Suddenly the sky seemed bluer, everyone around us seemed to be smiling, and my heart started banging in my chest as if it was about to escape altogether.

'Are we really?' I tried to sound casual, but my voice went a bit squeaky. Kieran leaned across and kissed the tip of my nose. I swear, I almost fainted!

'Well, I hope so. Will you go out with me, Lainey?'

Now, you have to understand something very important. Although most of my year go out with someone different every week (it gets very confusing!), I've never had lovelorn suitors exactly *swarming* around me. The other boys I've been out with (well, just one boy actually, Luke Ashton) didn't really ask me out. He just danced with me a few times (he was a terrible dancer, an arm-flinger) and told everyone else he was going out with me. And that was that. He didn't even offer to walk me home. I saw him a week later at youth club and he ignored me. Dianne said that he'd told her he had dumped me in favour of Iris Snell. Nice of him to keep me informed, wasn't it? So this was the first time I'd been officially Asked Out, and boy, was I happy!

'Yes!' I said, trying to resist the urge to dance wildly around the courtyard.

So there you have it, from the horse's mouth, so to speak. I was going out with luscious Kieran Kamau, the BOMD! Apart from trying not to think about Mum's Big Decision I'd never been so happy in my entire *life*!

Chapter Ten

Family Conference

When I arrived home at my curfew, 8.30 p.m. (well, it's actually 8 pm, but I figured Mum owed me some leeway), a post-it note with 'Precipitation' was stuck to the inside of the front door. Mum, Aunt Carol, Aunt Bee, and Uncle Denny were all sitting around the dining table. The pink fluffy cloud I'd been floating on with Kieran all afternoon came crashing around my ankles and threatened to trip me up. They all looked serious. Aunt Carol looked as if she might blow a gasket at any moment (a bit like Dad in the lift, really), and was having a rant about insanity in the family, and trying to waft the smoke from Aunt Bee's cigarette away. She hates smokers. Aunt Bee was gesticulating madly, as usual, almost poking Aunt Carol in the eye with her cigarette and laughing a bit hysterically, and Uncle Denny looked a bit shell-shocked and was very, very quiet. Mum was unusually, chillingly, calm. She just nodded at me when I strolled in, and told me that there was some rice and cheese bake and salad in the fridge for me. Suddenly I didn't feel at all hungry. I stood in the doorway, scowling.

'Lainey, take your meal upstairs. We're talking,' Mum said firmly. I went and sat between Aunt Bee and Uncle Denny at the table. 'Lainey, *out*!' Mum said *very* forcefully. I shook my head and stayed put. 'Lainey, we are having a private conversation,' Mum said, frowning her Demon Mother frown at me. I didn't move. Aunt Bee took another puff of her cigarette and blew a smoke ring.

'She has a right to be here,' she told Mum. 'This concerns her.' I leaned against Aunt Bee and twiddled a curl of her hair around my finger. I really am very fond of Aunt Bee. Mum sighed.

Aunt Carol glared at Mum. 'Ellen, I don't approve of this at all. Look, Todd and I can lend you some money.' Mum shook her head. Sometimes, especially when she's with Aunt Carol, she reminds me of me when I'm in a rebellious mood.

'It's all arranged,' she insisted.

'What's arranged?' I asked. The sinking feeling in my stomach was getting worse by the second.

'It can be un-arranged,' Uncle Denny told her.

'Yes. Un-arrange it. I mean, just cancel it,' said Aunt Carol. Aunt Bee stubbed out her cigarette, lit another, and went into the kitchen. She came straight back with a bottle of wine and some glasses, and started pouring and handing them round. I didn't get one.

Mum shook her head just as I asked *what* had been arranged. And the Awful News was disclosed.

I've told you that Mum's eccentric and has idiosyncrasies. Well, now I'm telling you that without any doubt at all she is bonkers, nuts, certifiably barking mad. She has Idiotsyncrasies.

Mum's plan was to rent out the house (she'd already found some people who needed a place to stay for three months, then intended to put the house with an estate agent after they'd left) and to move to a Community in the country in deepest Nottinghamshire. With me. A Community full of weirdo strangers who grow vegetables and keep livestock and whose children don't go to school. She's spoken to the people there, and we'd be moving in a week. A *week*! Mum described it as if it was the most exciting news imaginable, and that she expected me to be thrilled to bits. For once I was too shocked to even speak. My mouth opened and closed a few times, like a fish that's been pulled out of the water and is drowning in air. In fact I wished I was a fish, so that I could swim away and never have to see her again. How could she *do* this to me? In that moment I actually hated her.

Of course, I told her that no way was I going there. I told her I'd move in with Dad, even if he doesn't want me around. She patiently explained that Dad was in no position to take me on. I begged Aunt Bee and Uncle Denny to let me live with them, and Aunt Bee put her arms around me while I sobbed and hiccoughed and raged, and reminded me that both of them go away a lot with their work, so I couldn't stay with them full-time. I insisted that I'd move in with Amy, or even (Heaven help me, I really was desperate) with Dianne and The Hordes. I'd willingly make the sacrifice of having my clothes 'borrowed' to stay in Bath.

Through all this Aunt Carol was tight-lipped. When I stopped to draw breath and blow my nose she turned to Mum and said, 'Now, Ellen, look what you've done. The poor child is distraught.' For the first time in ages I actually liked Aunt Carol, and asked whether I could live with her and Uncle Todd. She took a deep, deep breath and stood up.

'Ellen,' she said, picking up her handbag, 'there's no reasoning with you.' And she left without answering my question.

Chapter Eleven

The Pits

Of course, I burbled out everything about the BOMD, and how I couldn't leave my home and my friends, especially now that I had found The One. Aunt Bee clucked and sympathised. Uncle Denny smiled sympathetically at me and then glared at Mum. Mum looked a bit surprised, and said that 'absence makes the heart grow fonder.' I swore. Mum told me off. I jumped up, knocking Aunt Bee's wineglass to the floor (it didn't break, unfortunately, but the wine spilled), and ran out of the door and straight to Amy's before Mum could grab me.

Amy and her parents were out. I sat on the step for a few minutes, then realised that I was a sitting duck if Mum came looking for me, so I went around the side of the house and sat in the back garden instead. After a while I heard someone going up the front path, and was just about to go around in case it was Amy when the person knocked on the door. I hid in the bushes by the back door, and, sure enough, heard Mum calling my name. I squirmed further into the bushes. Mr Smith, the big orange cat, came into the garden and miaowed at me. I put my finger on my lips and tried to telepathically instruct him to be quiet. Mum's footsteps pattered around the path and then stopped. 'Lainey?' she called. I held my breath, and after a minute she turned and left. I breathed deeply, and Mr Smith wound himself around my legs and purred.

By the time Amy and her parents came home it was very dark, and I was cold and hungry. I waited for a while longer, until the light went on in Amy's bedroom, then threw some pebbles at her window. It opened and Amy peeked out.

'Lainey, is that you?' she hissed.

'Yes.' I tried for a loud whisper.

'Wait there,' she said. A couple of minutes later the back door opened and she came outside, calling for Mister Smith. I made a 'Pssst' sound and she raced over to the bushes. I just couldn't help it. I started to cry again, and told Amy about Mum's Big Decision. Just as she was giving me a hug a shadow appeared in front of us and made me jump. It was Amy's mum. She took my arm in a vice-like grip, led me into the kitchen, with Amy trailing behind us, and gave me a royal telling-off about upsetting my mother. Apparently Mum had left a frantic message on their answerphone. When I explained, she let me sit down and gave me some juice while she went to phone Mum to tell her I was safe, and that they'd bring me home soon. After that she seemed quite sympathetic, and even patted my hand and said that things would work out. Then she took me home.

Aunt Bee and Uncle Denny were still there, and they told me off, too, for upsetting Mum. No one seemed to care much about how upset I am because she was *ruining* my life! Mum sent me straight to my room, but she brought some food up for me later on. I pretended to be asleep, so she left it and tiptoed out.

When I went downstairs in the morning, deliberately making my uniform look as scruffy as possible, there were empty boxes and filled bin-bags in the living room, and Mum was dragging a mattress into the garden. I peeked in one of the bin-bags. All my old clothes and toys from when I was young were stuffed inside. Mum came back dusting her hands together and smiled at me, but her smile wasn't real. It didn't reach her eyes.

'What are you doing with my stuff?' I asked, hating it that my voice sounded higher than usual, as if looking at my childhood thrown into a bin-bag had turned me back into a seven-year-old.

Mum sighed. 'Oh Lainey,' she said, 'You outgrew all those things years ago. They're going to the charity shop.'

I started to pull everything out. Tiny clothes, dolls, and jigsaw puzzle pieces flew across the room. 'Over my dead body,' I shrieked. 'That's my *past* you're throwing away!'

'But Lainey ...' Just then the phone rang. Mum picked it up. 'Hello?' she said tentatively. 'Oh, yes. Just a moment. Lainey, it's for you.' She handed the receiver over. When I heard Kieran's voice I dropped the doll I was clutching. He sounded cheerful and chirpy, and invited me over to his house after school!

I won't repeat the row that Mum and I had before I went upstairs to get ready for school, because I said some things that I felt a bit mean about later on. But it was her fault for provoking me.

Chapter Twelve

Kieran

Kieran must have been lurking right next to the door, because he opened it as soon as I rang the bell. I must admit that I was impressed by the house. It's right beside the park, and it's absolutely vast! There's a big staircase, and downstairs rooms leading off a lobby that's big enough to fit a classroom in. I half-expected a butler to appear, like in the old films, with a silver tray and iced drinks, but no one did. Kieran took me into the kitchen, which was huge, and introduced me to his mum, Estelle. She was taking a cake out of the oven, and I could feel my jaw drop to my knees. Estelle was beautiful! She was very tall, even taller than me (so that's where Kieran gets his height), and had dark hair, which was twisted up in a chignon. I just couldn't help asking how she did it like that (the words slipped out before I could stop them), and, in a husky voice with a French accent, she offered to show me how to do it later on. I was thrilled!

Kieran's dad was working in his study so we peeked around the door and I felt quite shy when he invited us in. His study has bookshelves lining all the walls, and a big, dark wooden desk with a state-of-the-art computer and lots of bits of paper on it. There was stained glass in the windows, and a tall African wooden statue in one corner. I thought a tap was running somewhere, then realised that there was a small fountain in the room. Kieran's dad, who's called Thomas, noticed me looking at it and explained that he finds the sound of water helps him to focus while he's writing. Thomas is even taller than Kieran and Estelle, and quite solidly built. His skin is very dark, like chocolate, and his eyes are almost black and very twinkly. I felt

43

a bit awe-struck by both Kieran's parents, and by his house. It's almost a mansion. But they were both very nice to me, and I wished I had parents as cool as them. Lucky Kieran – no wonder he seems so confident.

We went upstairs to Kieran's room. I couldn't help touching everything, and Kieran thought it was really funny. The room was more than twice the size of my room, and a lot of it was full of music stuff – amps, a mixer, an electric guitar, and a huge stereo system, as well as record decks. He has a double bed which I tried not to look at, (but I can tell you that it had a dark maroon duvet cover, and it had cushions scattered around on top of it, like something from the *Arabian Nights* stories! His parents must be very rich) and an armchair that Kieran guided me towards. I felt as if I was losing the power of speech again, but he started telling me about his band in London (they're called Dark Matter), and plugged his guitar in and played a lead guitar riff. It was amazing! I wanted to swoon. In fact, I nearly did swoon.

Then the best thing in my entire life happened. He sang, and his voice made my insides turn to jelly. When Kieran talks he sounds, well, normal. He has quite a deep voice. But when he sings it sounds as if someone has poured honey over gravel. I know that sounds weird, but it's true. A part of me was dissolving into the chair, while the rest of me wanted to leap up and dance. The song was about love at first sight, and it had a strong, thumping rhythm but was really romantic at the same time. I was awestruck.

When he stopped and looked at me to gauge my reaction I couldn't remove the huge grin from my face. I just sat, feeling hypnotised, and *beamed*. 'What do you think?' he asked, seeming a bit anxious.

'I think that's the most amazing music I've ever heard!' I told him. 'Wow! What a voice! Whose song is it?'

Kieran relaxed, I could tell because his shoulders dropped, and put the guitar back on its stand. 'Glad you like it, because I wrote that song for you.'

Of course, it would be nice to say that I was cool and casual, and acted as if a BOMD wrote amazing songs for me every day.

But I wasn't. My heart actually stopped for a moment, then gave a funny little bump before it started beating again (though much, much faster than usual). I squeaked, and could feel my eyes popping out and my jaw dropping in a very unattractive manner. Then I just stared at him.

'For me? You really wrote that song? And you wrote it for *me*?'

Kieran nodded and sat on the edge of the chair, smiling broadly.

'That's the most wonderful thing anyone's done for me in my *whole life*,' I said. And then he kissed me.

Chapter Thirteen

First Kiss

I've read somewhere that you never forget your first kiss. But I didn't expect it to be quite so embarrassing. It started off beautifully, like something out of a Hollywood movie. I suddenly realised that Kieran's face was coming closer to mine, and I knew, just *knew*, that he was going to kiss me. My heart blooped again, and I raised my face to meet him halfway because I really, really wanted to kiss him too. But somehow it didn't work like it does in the films. I put my head at the wrong angle and Kieran's chin collided with my nose, which hurt a bit and made me giggle nervously. He drew back slightly, and I felt utterly mortified, and thought he'd changed his mind forever. But Kieran ignored my giggles and swooped down very quickly so that our mouths actually connected that time.

Our teeth bumped together a bit, which made me want to giggle again, and that came out as a sort of 'smrrrgh' sound because, of course, there was nowhere for the giggle to go. Then all I was aware of was how good his lips felt, soft and warm and cushiony, and it made me feel tingly all over. That kiss was the one to *really* remember! It went on for ages, until we were both a bit breathless, and it only stopped when Estelle called us.

We leaped apart very quickly in case she came in, and then walked down the stairs together, trying to look as if nothing had happened, which was actually quite difficult because our faces were a bit pink, and my knees were definitely wobbling. Estelle had laid the table in their dining room and it was like nothing, I mean *nothing*, that we've ever had at home! The room was huge (all their rooms seemed to be huge), and there was a massive table covered in a white lace tablecloth, and eight carved chairs, and the table was laden with food! Vols-au-vent with teeny pieces of mushroom poking out of the tops, tiny little sandwiches, little glass bowls filled with olives and crisps and nuts. And the cake, the *piece de resistance* as Estelle called it! While we were upstairs, Estelle had covered it with icing, and piped on little spirals and hearts, and there was a real rose blossom in the centre. What with all that and the kissing, I thought I must have died and gone to Fairyland!

Estelle told us to sit down, and Kieran poured us some juice into real wine glasses from a crystal jug. I just sat and feasted my eyes on it all until Kieran put his hand under the tablecloth and squeezed my hand. That made me jump, but I squeezed back as if this was completely normal behaviour and I did that sort of thing all the time. When Estelle, chattering away, filled a plate and took it through to Thomas, Kieran leaned across and kissed me again. We quickly separated when we heard Estelle coming back.

It was the best evening I'd ever had. Estelle was so friendly and warm, but not embarrassing like my mum. She didn't ask about school like most adults do. She asked lots of questions about my favourite places and what I love doing most. (I did confess to my fondness for daisy chains and caricatures). And she told me all about when she used to be a model, trippy-tripping along catwalks at all the famous shows. She says that models have to be tall, like me, which made me glow a bit. Kieran is obviously proud of her, because he told her to fetch some magazines with photos of her on the cover, and she looked amazing all made up and wearing designer clothes.

And all the time we were talking, Kieran's foot was nudging against mine, and mine was nudging him back. Kieran told his mum that he'd written a new song just for me, and she said that he is very lucky to have a muse. Then later she showed me how to put my hair in a chignon, and Kieran took me upstairs and played My Song again. And we did lots more kissing.

When we walked home together I started to cry, because I didn't want to leave Kieran, or Amy, or even Kieran's mum. I wished she was my mum, but then realised that if she was, he'd be my brother and we couldn't kiss, so that changed my mind for me. I told Kieran about being dragged away to the Middle of Nowhere in a week, and he looked very upset and hugged me very tightly. Then he said I must come and stay with them as often as I can, and that he would visit me in deepest Nottinghamshire.

'Lainey,' he said, looking into my eyes, 'You will still be my girlfriend, wherever you are.'

But it's not the same as being here.

Chapter Fourteen

Goodbyes

A week had never flown by so fast. All my friends were as upset as me, and promised to text and Skype me every single day. I cried a lot and refused to pack and to eat anything, and I ripped up Mum's WOD every time I saw one. Every time Mum spoke to me I just gave her the Killer Glare that I'd learned from Dianne, and stormed out of the room. I ignored Mum's red eyes, and pretended not to hear her crying in her room every night. I just told myself that it was all her fault that we were going away.

On my last day at school I drew caricatures of all the teachers during the lessons, and stuck them up on the notice board, but no one told me off. People bought presents for me. Dianne gave me a friendship bracelet, and so did Hannah. Rosa gave me a little necklace with an 'L' for Lainey on it. Amy cried all day and said she'd come round in the morning to say goodbye properly. And Kieran, who I had snuck out to meet every day after school, walked me home and insisted on coming in to speak to Mum, even though I told him she didn't deserve to ever be spoken to again, by anyone.

Mum looked pleased when we walked in, I'd refused to let her meet Kieran, so she seemed to think it was a truce at last. I didn't say one single word to her, but Kieran was very polite. He introduced himself and told her that I was invited to stay anytime. He looked away from the pathetic little pile of belongings in the corner of the room (Mum wanted to travel light), and he didn't even raise an eyebrow at the WOD that was posted on the mantelpiece (it was 'disseminated', if you must know). Mum said she may let me visit after I have settled in, but that I have to make my home at the Community first. I stormed out, and Kieran politely said goodbye to Mum and followed me. We kissed at the gate, and I watched him walk away until he disappeared around the corner. I really, truly felt my heart breaking into little pieces.

The next morning, Mum loaded our stuff into the car and wedged Horace's cage in between the bags on the back seat. Horace twitched his whiskers and looked as worried as I felt, then went and hid in his bed. I wished I could do the same. Amy came round very early and gave me a book about best friends, and a package that was all wrapped in glittery paper. She whispered that it was her special hair straighteners, and that made me cry even more. I gave her my floaty blue top that looks so pretty on her, and a bracelet with shells on it that I got from the charity shop, and a daisy chain that I'd made for her. She promised to keep it forever, even when it's all dried out and brown. We both hugged and cried, and Mum had to tell me about fifty times to get in the car. In the end she took my arm and forced me into the back seat, next to Horace's cage, and I turned around and waved to Amy until I couldn't see her any more.

My WOD is 'devastated.'

Chapter Fifteen

Ivy House

As soon as we left Bath, I closed my eyes so that I wouldn't see us going further and further away. After a while I did actually fall asleep, and I didn't wake up until Mum shook my arm and said that we had arrived. I sat up and looked out of the window.

We were right outside a huge old manor house all covered with ivy. It looked very creepy. I could see nothing but trees and green fields everywhere, not another house in sight. We were at the end of a long driveway that turned into a circle in front of the house. Mum stepped out of the car and opened my door. Resigned, I checked on Horace, who was still asleep, stretched, and got out, and we both stood looking at the sign on the big front door. It said Ivy House. The people who named it clearly had very little imagination.

Mum lifted the big knocker (there didn't seem to be a doorbell), and we could hear it echo, like something out of a horror movie. Then two *huge,* grey wolf-like dogs, all teeth and legs and fur, came hurtling around the side of the house and jumped up at us, barking and slavering. They were as tall as me when they stood on their hind legs, and I was so petrified that I was frozen to the spot! Mum made ineffectual noises and almost fell over when one put its paws on her shoulders and licked her face. Then the door opened, and the dogs ran inside, tails wagging. I didn't want to see what kind of awful monster was going to appear next, so I looked at Mum. She looked scared, but she smiled at me. I did my disdainful lip-lift (you just raise one corner of your mouth, and scowl a bit, if you want to try it yourself).

'Greetings! You must be Ellen and Lainey!' Greetings? Who

says that nowadays? I kept my disdainful lip-lift intact and took a good look at our new housemate. He was quite short (well, shorter than me), with long, wavy, fair hair that reached almost to his waist. His chin and cheeks were all stubbly, and he was wearing baggy workmen's dungarees (dungarees? I couldn't believe my eyes!). His eyes were crinkly, so I guessed that he smiled a lot.

The man stepped aside to let us in. 'I'm Dom,' he said, and hugged Mum. I mean, here we were, with a stranger, and he hugged her! He tried to hug me too, but I sidestepped very quickly and he missed. Mum looked a bit taken aback by the hug, but gave him a little pat on the arm to show that she was friendly.

Dom took us into a big square hallway. There was quite a lot of mud on the floor. A shriek made me jump, and I looked up to see a very small child of indeterminate sex sliding at great speed down the banisters, followed close behind by someone of eleven or twelve who I guessed was probably a boy by the way it was shouting. They both wore jeans and T-shirts, and had long, tangled hair, and they landed, laughing, in a heap on the floor right in front of us. Dom grinned and helped the Small Child to its feet.

'Bryony, Leila, meet our new Community members,' he said jovially, as if it was perfectly normal to slide down bannisters. I looked at them. They looked at me. So they were both girls. The Small Child took my hand.

'Will you come and swing on the rope with me?' she asked.

Dom laughed. 'Leila, this is Ellen, and this is Lainey. She'll play with you in a while, but you can help me show them around if you like.'

Now let me get this straight, immediately. I was not in the habit of playing with small children, let alone going through the gross indignity of swinging from ropes like a monkey. I tried to ignore the sticky little hand that clutched mine like a vice, and glanced at the other girl. Bryony. She looked very much like a boy to me, apart from her long hair. Though, as Dom's hair was even longer, I guessed I could be in for a hard time gauging the genders around here. Bryony stared at me curiously, taking in my make-up and my ultra-short T-shirt, and sniffed then walked away without saying a word. That particular native certainly didn't seem friendly.

Mum bent down to Leila's level. 'How old are you, Leila?' she asked. The Small Child let go of my hand and clutched Mum's instead.

'I'm three,' she told Mum proudly, and we followed Dom to a doorway that led into the biggest, untidiest kitchen I have ever seen in my life. It had a huge range in it, covered in pans, lots of cupboards, boxes all over the floor, a big, very tatty table, and more inhabitants, who were sitting around drinking from large mugs. They stopped talking when we came in, and shuffled around to offer extra space on the benches around the table. Reluctantly I squeezed in beside Mum and the small child, while Dom provided the introductions. The wolfish dogs were lying by the range, and their tails slapped the ground when we came in, but (thankfully) they didn't get up.

There were two women and two men. Aileen was (I guessed) in her late twenties and quite pretty, with very short, spiky, very red hair (I immediately deduced that it was definitely not naturally red, because bits of colour had stained her skin around the hairline). She had such an infectious grin that I almost smiled back, but caught myself just in time. The other woman, Sarah, was about Mum's age (thirty-eight) and she had dreadlocks to her waist, with bits of coloured wool in them. She had lived there the longest, along with Tink, who sat next to her.

Tink is a man. I *know*, I was shocked, too! You'd think someone called that would be named after Tinkerbell from *Peter Pan*, but apparently he got his name because he's good at tinkering with bits of machinery. Then there was Lincoln, who I didn't like at all, because he looked at my chest before looking at my face. People who do that give me the shudders. Lincoln was old, probably in his forties at least, and had a bandana around his head and strands of grey hair poking out of the back and sides.

Mum said hello to everyone in turn, repeating their names so that she'd remember them. Sarah poured some tea from a pot and gave us a mug each, except that when I looked at it, it wasn't real tea at all. It was murky coloured herbal tea that Sarah said was made with fresh herbs from the garden. My heart had sunk so low by then that I thought it must be somewhere close to the Earth's core.

They explained that the Community is mostly self-sufficient, and that they get extra income from groups of people staying there to do courses. Then Sarah showed us The List. The List is a rota of all the chores that have to be done by everyone. As she went through it with us, my heart sank to the approximate vicinity of the next galaxy along from us. Cleaning (including the toilets), washing, gardening, cooking, washing up (the messy sink made me wonder who was shirking on their chores), child-care, husbandry (no, that's nothing to do with marriage, it's looking after the animals), mending, repairs, herb preparation, composting, cheese-making, looking after guests. It went on. And on. And on. I tuned out until I noticed Mum give an envelope to Sarah.

'What's in there?' I asked loudly. Mum shushed me. Sarah looked at me.

'It's your contribution towards your keep,' she said.

'But if we're working here, doing animal husbandry and cleaning toilets, why do we have to pay?' I asked. I thought that was a very reasonable question, but Mum shushed me again.

Sarah sighed, and put the envelope in a big tin on one of the shelves. 'We all pay our way here,' she declared sanctimoniously. I turned to Mum.

'But I thought we'd moved here so that you wouldn't be paying out lots of money!'

Dom stood up. 'Come. Let me show you to your sleeping quarters.' I swear he thinks he's from another century. We followed him out, back into the hallway, with the Small Child still gripping Mum's hand as though she belonged to us.

Chapter Sixteen

It Gets Worse

I was now officially at rock bottom. Mum's room was over the opposite side of the building. It reminded me of a tiny cell. My sleeping place was far from where the adults are, presumably so they're not disturbed by children making a noise. My 'bedroom' was a dormitory. Yes, it's true. I was taken to a huge, dark room high up in the attics, with small, prison-like windows, a huge old fireplace that Dom said didn't actually work any more, two sets of bunk beds, and two single beds. As a new resident I was allocated a single bed, and I got the impression it was something I should be grateful for.

I looked around. The fireplace was clearly a hunting ground for spiders. It was dark and dusty, and there was a little pile of soot in the grate, as if something had flown down and landed there. It made me shudder. The beds looked old (apparently most of the furniture here is recycled), and I wondered how many people had died in the one I'd be sleeping in. The windows were too narrow to escape from, and too high up – unless you were Rapunzel and could let down your mile of hair to use as a rope. Mine isn't quite long enough for that yet. The walls were grey brick, and the only splashes of colour came from patchwork quilts and some drawings (presumably by the Small Child) that were stuck on nails on the walls. I glared at Mum. She didn't look terribly impressed either, but she put on her cheerful voice and suggested we bring our stuff inside and get settled. The Small Child finally let go of Mum's hand and bounced on the bottom bunk bed closest to 'my' bed, squealing like a mad creature. I decided to stay very quiet and plot my escape.

Just then Bryony came charging in, closely followed by an

older girl and a boy around my age. I deduced that he was a boy because he had big feet. They all had long hair, and they all looked scruffy and hostile. Dom introduced the newcomers as Pixie (the girl, who's sixteen), and Sparrow (the boy, who's fifteen). They all eyed me up and down as if I'd come from another planet, which I guess was probably an accurate assessment, and I gathered that Sparrow had the other single bed and the girls had the bunks. We had to share our bedroom with a *boy*! Yuck! I was sure that was illegal or something!

Sparrow was the only one who made any effort to be friendly, though. He offered to help bring our stuff upstairs, though I insisted on carrying Horace's cage. My rat seemed to be the only friend I had left in the world, and he woke up and poked his nose out of his nest just as I put his cage down beside my bed. The others all crowded round, staring. Sparrow looked at Horace, then at me.

'You keep a *rat* as a pet?' He seemed a bit bemused. I nodded, and opened the cage door. Horace ran up my arm and sat on my shoulder, doing his rat whisper in my ear while I stroked him. Sparrow stared at Horace. 'Rats are vermin,' he said.

I decided that, even though Sparrow had been quite helpful, I didn't like him at all.

A gong sounded downstairs, making me jump so that Horace nearly fell off my shoulder. The others galloped off, except for Sparrow, who was still staring at Horace in a way I didn't like one bit. 'We have to go down for dinner,' he told me, and turned away.

I put Horace back in his cage and fed him, then pushed his cage as far under my bed as it would go. Somehow I had a feeling that he wouldn't be very safe all alone up here.

Chapter Seventeen

The Dark Ages

Dinner was some kind of stew, and it wasn't vegetarian. Apparently the wolf-like dogs (which apparently are Lurchers, a mixture of Greyhounds and Wolfhounds), help Creepy Lincoln to hunt rabbits, and they'd caught some today. The thought of sweet little murdered bunnies in my stew made me feel really, really ill. Mum hesitantly told the Community that we were vegetarian, and Sarah breezily informed her that no special meals were provided, and we could pick out the meat for the dogs to eat later. I put my fork down and sat in silence throughout the meal, ignoring the glares of the younger members of the Community. Sparrow reached over and helped himself to the meat from my plate, saying he'd rather eat it than give it to the dogs. Clearly I was going to starve to death here, which seemed a brighter prospect than having to live here for ever and ever.

I was allocated washing-up duties after dinner, even though I hadn't eaten a thing. Pixie did the drying up, and the only time she spoke to me was to say that I'd better let go of my high principles. I ignored her.

Afterwards I asked Dom how I could access the internet on my phone, so that I could talk to my friends on Skype. Dom laughed as if I'd said something really, really funny.

'Lainey, we don't have computers here. Or a television. Or a phone. It's a technology-free zone. I can give you some recycled paper if you want to write letters, though.'

I glared at him, trying very, very hard not to cry. 'So how are those delivered? Pigeon post?' I asked. He just laughed and ruffled my hair as if I was a Small Child, so I stormed off.

My heart by then had sunk as far down as the cosmic dust that issued from the Big Bang. Even though it was almost dark, I went outside and sat in the gardens under a tree, as far from all of them as I could possibly get, while I tried fruitlessly to get a signal on my mobile. Clearly I didn't go far enough, though, because one of the Lurchers, the fatter one (they were both skinny, but her tummy was bigger), came and sat next to me, then put her head in my lap. I gave her head a stroke, and she gave a groan of bliss and closed her eyes. Her fur was surprisingly soft, and I actually felt quite comforted by her presence, even though it made me shudder to think that she killed poor little rabbits.

'Her name's Daisy. The other dog, her mate, is Skye.'

I jumped, and looked up. The dog thumped her tail but stayed where she was. Aileen sat down next to me, and placed a little wad of paper and a pen on the ground beside me. I glanced down to check whether it was a quill pen, as that wouldn't have surprised me, but it was a cheap biro.

'For letter-writing. This must all be very strange for you, Lainey, but you'll get used to it,' she told me. I glared at her.

'I don't want to get used to it. I want to go home.'

Aileen smiled, and leaned over to stroke Daisy's back. Daisy gave another blissful groan, and burrowed her head further into my lap.

'This is your home now. You'll settle in, but you need to make an effort, you know. We'll make allowances for you, but do try to be friendly, hon.'

I looked at her. She had a kind face, and I got the impression she really was trying to be helpful. 'This is not my home, and it never will be. I don't belong here,' I said.

Aileen got to her feet, leaving the paper with me, and Daisy stood and stretched, then shook herself. 'If you need a friend to talk to, come and find me.' She strolled off, with Daisy loping along at her heels. My lap felt cold and empty all of a sudden, so I went to the dormitory to cuddle Horace and write letters to Amy and Kieran, telling them that I had been thrust back into the Dark Ages and needed help to return to the Real World.

Chapter Eighteen

The Crying Girl

It was really, really weird going to bed that night. I was used to sleeping on my own (apart from having Horace around, of course!), or just sharing a room with friends. I had never, ever been as embarrassed and mortified as I was that first night (though it never did get easier, that really was The Pits).

They all sleep in their underwear – no pyjamas or anything! And they didn't seem at all bothered about being in a mixed room. I crept off to the bathroom (archaic, believe me!) to take my make-up off and put my pyjamas on, and fumbled my way back along the long corridor in the dark, feeling my way along the walls towards the dull glow of the lamp in the dormitory. The others were talking, but they went quiet when they heard me coming back. I ignored them and took Horace out of his cage so that he could cuddle up with me. He could nibble holes in these sheets to his heart's content as far as I was concerned. Pixie switched the lamp off, and made some comment about me sleeping with rats, and they all sniggered except for the Small Child, who tried to get into bed with me. I blocked her entrance and told her to sleep in her own bed, and she snuffled a bit but went away.

It was very, very dark. And colder indoors than outside. And scary. The others went to sleep quickly but I lay awake for hours, listening to all the strange noises and trying to figure out what they were. In fact, I wasn't sure whether I slept at all, and whether what happened next was real or a dream. I was lying quietly, with Horace tucked up beside my neck, slipping into that strange in-between state when you're not asleep but not fully awake, when everything suddenly went very, very weird.

'Help me! Let me out!'

The voice echoes through my head as if it's coming from somewhere deep inside me. But it's not my voice. It sounds like a girl with a funny accent, and her voice is sharp with terror. I sit up in bed, shivering, and move Horace close to the wall so that I won't squash him.

'Help me! Please, someone help me!'

I look across at the shapes of the others, barely discernible in the dark. No one is moving. It's not one of them.

The walls suddenly seem thin, then transparent, and the room is filled with a pale cold light, like at full moon. I can see all the way through into the next room, which just has some empty beds and a chest of drawers in it. But the wall opposite me has a space inside it next to the fireplace. And curled up in that space is a girl, not much older than me. She's wearing a thin cotton nightie. I think it's a nightie. She can see me, too. She's looking straight at me, and she's crying.

'Let me out! Please! Please help me!'

My heart is beating so fast that I can hardly breathe. I get out of bed and feel the cold floor under my feet. If this is a dream, it's the most vivid dream I've ever had. I walk across to the transparent wall. The girl's looking straight at me as if she can see me, and she's crying and crying.

I put out my hands to help pull her through into the room, but as soon as my fingers touch the wall it goes solid and she disappears. I call out, and find myself standing beside the fireplace, both hands flat against the stones.

Believe me, I was shivering so much by then that I truly thought I'd expire. I crept back into bed, pulled the ancient patchwork quilt over my head, and reached around for Horace, who was curled up fast asleep. I lay there until the sky got light, then put Horace back in his cage, pulled my clothes on very, very quietly, and, heart beating at double-time, crept out to look in the room next door in case the girl was there. It was filled with boxes and junk, and the dust was so thick that I could see my own footprints. There was no evidence that anyone had been in there for a long time. I went to sit outside under what I already thought of as 'my' tree. The dogs heard me moving around and followed me outside. I was quite grateful for their company, though I hoped no rabbits would be out so early in the morning.

There seemed no point in telling anyone about the crying girl, or the dream, or whatever it was. Who could I trust here? But it happened night after night, until I was so tired that I looked like a panda.

Chapter Nineteen

Shared Ownership

Every time I thought things surely couldn't get any worse, they did. I hardly saw Mum (not that I liked her at all – it's all her fault we're here), because she was always being dragged off to do animal husbandry, or weed the vegetables, or skin rabbits. She was actually sick the first few times she had to do that – Pixie told me with such scorn in her voice that I hit her, and she hit me back even harder, and then Aileen came and stepped calmly in between us without saying a word, and Pixie walked away.

There are lots of animals at the Community. The two Lurchers, of course. Several cats, which are kept for ratting and not as pets (that really worries me about Horace, so I daren't carry him around on my shoulder like I used to). A few goats and sheep. Chickens for eggs and for eating (I was getting thinner and thinner, because I refused to eat anything that was contaminated with meat). Cows for milk and cheese (the milk is drunk from jugs, warm and frothy, straight from the cows, and we churned it to make cheese and then had to put it through muslin strainers). Creepy Lincoln seemed to be in charge of the animal husbandry (in my opinion he'd never evolved even to the level of the animals, anyway), but everyone, including me, had to take their turn at feeding, brushing, milking, mucking out, churning, cheese-making. If my friends were here I would almost enjoy some of the tasks with the animals, because they're quite satisfying. I got close to Daisy and Skye very quickly – I think they sensed my sadness and made a big fuss of me to compensate for the horrible humans. But everyone was so vile that it was easier to go off on my own and get on with the work to be done.

Everyone had to do equal shares of the work (it takes up a lot of time), because none of the children have *ever* been to school. Never, ever!! I wondered how they'd managed to get away with that without the authorities stepping in, and I really never thought that the day would come when I would actually miss school, but I did. I felt as if my brain was just being filled with domestic stuff, and that all my paltry intelligence was putrefying like the slurry pit that really, really reeked across the other side of the fields.

I gradually learned more of the gazillions of rules here. One is that everything is Shared Ownership. This means that nothing belongs to anyone in particular. Everything is shared so that whoever wants it can have it. What a stupid idea! It meant that the people who were more forceful got everything, and the quiet ones (such as Mum) were left with the dregs. Her few pretty things, like a couple of treasured vases from her parents that she brought with her, were soon 'accumulated' for the Community. And though she said she didn't mind, she looked quite upset about it.

This also meant that what was mine was everyone else's. By day two all my make-up had disappeared, and Pixie was suddenly wearing eye shadow and blusher (she made a terrible job of putting it on, and looked like a clown!). And Leila and the Small Child could be seen wearing my T-shirts. Even Sparrow had one of them (it looked unbelievably silly on him). But this sharing of possessions didn't extend to me. My belongings disappeared into other people's piles, but no one else's found its way to mine. Not that I'd want to wear their clothes anyway. Only Horace was left in my charge, and I guarded him closely in case he vanished, too.

The mega-low point, though, was the letters.

I'd written long, rambling letters to Amy and Kieran, explaining about the Dark Ages and lack of phone and computers and TV, and the awful people, and the poisonous food, and the animals (I was nice about the dogs), but I didn't mention the Crying Girl in case they thought I'd completely lost

66

my marbles. They both wrote back straight away each time (though I had to wait a few days for the replies).

Amy gave me all the gossip – Dianne was going out with Todd Harvey (which made me laugh a bit because he made Spotty Scotty look like an Adonis!) and everyone was missing me lots, and she had my daisy chain up on the wall above her bed. That made me cry, because I missed her so much.

Kieran wrote to say that he missed me lots, too, and that he'd been writing some new songs for me. He sent the lyrics for one of them, and three whole lines of kisses at the end of his letter, and Estelle put a pretty card in for me. That made me cry even more.

I kept the letters under my bed, next to Horace's cage, and got them out to read them at least ten times a day. Then they disappeared. I asked everyone, and searched everywhere, but never did find them. After that, all my letters were hidden away under a mattress in one of the unused bedrooms, and I made sure that no one saw me going in there. It meant I couldn't read them as often, but at least they were safe.

The other Major Rule that no one had enlightened us about initially was Shared Parenting. This meant that children were considered to be everyone's responsibility, not just their parents'. Pixie and Bryony were Sarah's children (no wonder Pixie was so snide and bossy, and Bryony was a bully), Sparrow was Tink's son, and Leila was Aileen's daughter, but the view was that all the adults were considered to be their parents. I know. I couldn't believe my ears either.

So Sarah would tell me off for not eating meat, and Mum wasn't allowed to step in. And Creepy Lincoln could stare at my chest as much as he wanted without anyone saying a word, but I was sent to my room if I called him a slimeball. He actually made me feel quite scared, and I was very, very careful to never be caught on my own when he was around.

Ironically, Mum seemed quite happy on the times when I did see her. I think she liked it that she didn't have full responsibility for me. And after a week or so I noticed her and Dom canoodling a few times, which was quite retch-worthy. It made me think of what she'd told me about the long-dead, long-haired rock star Marc Bolan, who she'd been in love with when she was even younger than me. As Dom had long hair, too, maybe he reminded her of her lost love.

So, between pining for my friends and the BOMD, realising to my horror that every day had become a BHD, feeling all alone in the cruel, cruel world (apart from Horace and the dogs), and enduring the cries of the ghost every night, life really did suck. And then something happened that was so unspeakably shocking that it galvanised me into immediate action.

Chapter Twenty

The Very, Very Last Straw

I wasn't very 'with it' that day, on account of no sleep for weeks because of the Crying Girl, and the enforced labour all day every day. I fed Horace a little bit of cheese (his favourite treat) when I got up, then put him in his cage with his breakfast and some fresh water. I stumbled through the day in a miserable haze, ignoring Pixie's pointed comments about my uselessness when I knocked the milk churn so that some was spilled, and slid away from Creepy Lincoln every time he came near me. I steered clear of the house guests who were doing a course in meditation over the other side of the house, and who seemed to think we were some sort of peep show. And in the evening I sat under 'my' tree with Skye, while everyone else in the Community swam naked in the pond at the bottom of the hill. No way was I getting involved in their weirdness, or jumping about without my clothes on! Their shouts and squeals echoed for miles.

When it got dark and the countryside was quiet I crept indoors and went up to bed, hoping that an early night would trick the Crying Girl into leaving me in peace. I pulled Horace's cage out from under my bed to take him out, and screamed and screamed. His cage door was open, and Horace was gone.

Mum and Aileen came rushing up the stairs, swiftly followed by Dom. I couldn't stop screaming, and Mum held me very, very tightly until I'd run out of screams and could only sob. Aileen looked at Horace's cage and said, very quietly, 'Oh dear.' We searched and searched, but there was no sign of him. Mum sat with me until I cried myself to sleep, but she must have tiptoed away because when I woke in the night, to the

Crying Girl's pleas, only the other kids were in the room. I peeked into Horace's cage in case he'd come back, but it was still empty. I never found out who had let him out, and all I could think about was poor Horace scared, cold, and alone, wondering why I hadn't come to rescue him. It was the absolute worst thing that had ever, ever happened to me.

I lay in bed for a while, trying to ignore the Crying Girl and crying along with her about the loss of my furry friend, when a thought occurred to me. I got dressed and crept downstairs. Daisy and Skye were lying by the range, and they thumped their tails when I went into the kitchen. I shushed them very softly and went to the high shelf where the money tin was kept, carefully lifted it down and opened it, keeping my ears cocked towards the door in case anyone appeared. For a Community that went on about the unimportance of money, there was quite a lot in there. I hesitated because, despite finding Dianne's Lipstick Incident very funny, I really do abhor stealing. Then I thought of Horace, and that made my mind up for me. I took the money, put it in the pocket of my jeans, and quietly let myself out through the back door. Then I ran as fast as I could, all the way to the main road.

It was miles to the nearest bus stop, and dawn was breaking as I got there. By then I wasn't running, but sort of staggering. I didn't have a clue how far we were from the nearest town, and I didn't know how long it would take before the money and I were missed, so I hid in the bushes for ages until *finally* a bus came along. I bought a ticket to the bus station (not knowing what town it was in, even!), and when I arrived there I went up to the ticket office and asked for the best route to Bath.

It took two more buses and a train, and it was already night time when the train pulled into Bath Spa station. I have never, *ever* been so happy to see a place in my whole life!

I took a bus to Amy's house and her face, when she opened the door, was such a picture of shock that, despite my heartbreak, I couldn't help laughing through my tears.

'I've run away,' I told her, as she dragged me inside to face the equally shocked expressions of her parents.

Chapter Twenty-one

Home Sweet Home

Amy's parents were extraordinarily kind. They took a good hard look at me and I suddenly saw how awful I must appear to them, with my filthy, scruffy clothes hanging off me, my thin, unmade-up face, straggly hair, and huge black shadows under my eyes. Amy's mum insisted on ordering a vegetarian takeaway meal for me, as they'd already eaten, and I had a veggie curry with rice and poppadums and naan bread, and banana fritters for afterwards. It was my first proper meal since we'd left Bath, despite all the vegetable tending I'd been doing, and I ate it at top speed. I had cola to drink, and Amy sat beside me holding my hand the whole time, so I ate everything one-handed, with a fork. She kept saying, 'What have they *done* to you?' And from the horrified expressions on her parents' faces, I guessed they were thinking the same thing. It was soooo good to feel surrounded by people who cared.

Afterwards I told them all that had been happening at Ivy House. Everything. The Crying Girl in the dormitory, the hostile Dorm Demons, the chores, the stolen letters, the dogs, Creepy Lincoln, Mum and Dom. And, finally, the disappearance of Horace. I cried so much over Horace that Amy cried with me (she loved Horace too) and her mum came over and gave me a big hug. She's not usually the huggy sort at all, but she looked as upset as I felt. I hugged her back.

Amy's dad, who is very practical, asked how much money I had 'borrowed' (that's how he put it, very tactfully), and said that he would reimburse it. Then the phone rang. It was Mum, ringing from the call-box in the village to ask whether anyone had heard from me. It had taken them a while to discover my absence, apparently. After everyone had moaned about me not being around to do my chores (they thought I'd wandered off to mourn Horace alone), Sarah realised about the missing money, and the inhabitants of Ivy House were in an uproar about it. Not about me being missing – about the money!

I refused to speak to Mum, but Amy's mum talked to her for a long, long time in private. She told me afterwards that I was allowed to stay with them for a week because school holidays had just started, but that I had to go back. I said that I'd rather die, and she told me that Mum would talk to the others and see what she could do to make life easier. I wasn't convinced, but Amy's mum said there was no choice, and to make the most of the next week.

Amy ran a hot bath for me, with lots of scented bubbles, and gave me a pair of her pyjamas (they were too short in the legs, but I didn't mind), and I fell asleep straightaway in the lovely familiar guest bed in her room, before she'd even got ready for bed herself. With friends around me, and no Crying Ghost, I slept for fifteen whole hours!

Chapter Twenty-two

In The Fold

Word had got out by the time I woke up at around midday the next day. Amy had texted *everyone* to say that I was with her. All my friends wanted to rush round immediately but Amy, being kind (and very thoughtful), suggested that we all meet in the park in the afternoon. She knew that I'd hate to be seen with messy hair, and scruffy clothes, and panda eyes.

So, when I woke she ran another bubble bath, and I washed my hair, and she showed me some T-shirts and a pair of jeans that her mum had gone out and bought while I was asleep. I cried a bit over how *nice* her parents are, and how *normal*. Then I put on the new clothes, and Amy straightened my hair (she had new straighteners, though the ones she gave me had been acquired elsewhere at the Community so I never got to use them). And she gave me a makeover, using lots of concealer under my eyes. Honestly, my black shadows were worse than Dianne's. By the time she'd finished I didn't look too bad, though every time I thought of Horace, and what would have been his dreadful fate, my eyes filled with tears again, and we had to start over. It took over two hours to make me presentable.

We all met up in Victoria Park at four o'clock. Dianne and Hannah and Rosa all rushed over and hugged me 'til I thought I'd suffocate, and I hugged them all back, ecstatic to be home again. Lots of other school friends were there, too, and even Spotty Scotty, who was still pink around the gills near Amy, but looked much less spotty than usual. Everyone had a glow around them, and I was sooo happy to see them! I wondered whether Kieran had decided not to come, and started to feel a bit sad, then heard an acoustic guitar playing round the corner by the duck pond. Amy and Dianne winked at me, and we all followed the sound. There, standing by the bridge over the pond, was Kieran. He looked unbelievably gorgeous, and he was singing 'my' song, and smiling at the same time. I ran, literally *ran*, over to him, and he dropped his guitar on the grass and gave me a *huge* hug. And a *very* long kiss. And everyone cheered and laughed.

We all went back to Kieran's for the evening and had a party. Estelle hugged me, too, when we arrived, and said that I must visit as often as I like. I was tempted to ask her whether I could move in with them, but thought that might be pushing my luck a bit too much, despite her hospitality.

Kieran played three new songs that he had written just for me, and everyone applauded and said that he was going to be a star. He really is brilliant (I would have said that even if the songs weren't for me). And suddenly it seemed that I was Very Cool for being Kieran's girlfriend, and having songs written and performed publicly for me, and for running away from a Very Traumatic Experience. I soaked up all the love, and tried not to think about having to go back. In fact, I tried not to think about Mum or Ivy House at all.

Chapter Twenty-two

Kieran

The next day was divided between Amy and Kieran. Amy's mum gave us some money so we went out round the charity shops in the morning. We bought a bright blue top for Amy, that I cut right back and re-stitched for her, and a green top for me. She looked really pretty in it when it was finished. In the afternoon we just lounged on her bed and did makeovers, and talked and talked.

Amy was still obsessed with John Carter, who had been out with (and subsequently dumped) three more girls since I went to Deepest Nottinghamshire. Amy thought she might have a chance of captivating and enchanting him, because he actually deigned to say hello to her last week, on his way past with another older beauty. I didn't want to disillusion her, because she's so lovely that any boy would be mad to ignore her, but I did express the opinion that she deserved to be with someone a little more *constant*. Amy just sighed, and said that the course of true love was often laden with rocks. Or was it pitfalls? Anyway, she meant that there were often challenges.

We talked a bit more about Ivy House. The thought of going back there filled me with deepest darkest horror, and really nothing that Amy said could help, so we went back to talking about boys. Amy told me that Kieran really had missed me, and that they both hung out together and talked about me a lot. Of course, I wanted to know *everything* that had been said and, fortunately, it was all nice.

Estelle had invited me to tea with them, and Kieran came to walk me there (how sweet!) at five o'clock. He was very polite to Amy's parents, and promised to bring me safely home later.

Amy's mum seemed very impressed by him, because she smiled a lot. Amy was going to youth club with Dianne and Hannah, so we arranged to meet them there later. Of course, the last time I went to youth club was the evening that Kieran and I first got together!

Estelle was very friendly, as always, and we chatted over tea (which was another amazing feast). Kieran had told her the sad story of Ivy House, and she was very shocked. She invited me to go and stay with them in a month, and said that if I tried very hard to fit in at Ivy House they might be kinder to me and let me go away sometimes. I couldn't imagine ever fitting in there, but I promised to do my best.

After the feast we went upstairs and kissed a lot, and Kieran played all his new songs to me. He had some Very Important News. That morning he'd had a phone call from someone at the *Teen Star* programme! He'd sent in a few of the songs he'd written with his London band, Dark Matter (and the first song he wrote for me, too!), and they wanted the band to go and audition for the programme *next week*!

Now, if you haven't heard of *Teen Star*, you must have been living somewhere like Ivy House, because it's *the* programme to watch! Every week they have five bands or solo singers, and the public votes for the one they like best. That band (or singer) is in the very last programme of each series, and the winner gets a recording contract and becomes very, very famous. And the BOMD was going to be in it!

I was so excited that I jumped all around the room. Then I realised that I wouldn't be here next week, and I almost cried. I told him that I'd go to the village phone box to call him and find out what happened. I knew, just *knew* that they would pass the audition!

Kieran hadn't told anyone except his parents and the band, because he wanted me to know before everyone else. I was very, very touched. We went to youth club, and then he told everyone. There was such an air of celebration that night that I couldn't bear to think I wouldn't be here for his audition. I tried not to think about Ivy House, though, and just enjoyed being with all my friends.

Kieran, Amy, and I walked back to her house together, arm in arm. It was a very warm feeling to be with the two people who I loved best in the world.

Chapter Twenty-four

Very, Very Good News

Amy's mum was watching out for us. It was easy to tell, because the curtains twitched and she opened the door before we even walked up the path. She had the biggest smile on her face! Before we could even say hello, her words came out in a big rush, tumbling over each other.

'Lainey! Your mother phoned, and she's found Horace!'

My heart gave a big thump.

'Is he alive?' I asked. Though I don't think she would have been smiling if he was dead, I didn't want to take anything for granted and get all upset again.

'Yes. Your mum's been looking for him ever since you left, and she found him huddled up in the back corner of the fireplace in the dormitory, all covered in soot. He's fine. She gave him a wash, and food and water, and he's in his cage in her room now.'

I couldn't help it. I just burst into tears, I was sooo relieved! My little Horace hadn't been eaten by a cat after all! Kieran and Amy hugged me and I hugged them back. Amy's mum patted my shoulder, then they both left Kieran and I on our own on the doorstep to say goodnight.

When I went inside a few minutes later, Amy and her mum were both beaming happily over the very, very, very good news. We sat on the sofa together, and I was smiling so much that I thought my teeth would fall out. I kept saying, 'He's alive! Horace is alive!' over and over again. I could hardly believe it! Then I would hug Amy, and she would hug me, then I'd say it again. And again.

'You know, Lainey,' Amy's mum murmured, 'your mum

really does love you. She kept on searching, even when it seemed that Horace wouldn't be found.'

I nodded. Even though I don't like Mum at all for dragging me to live in such a ghastly place, I had to admit that she'd really made a huge effort for me. It didn't make me want to go back there, but it did make me miss her just a *little* bit.

An awful thought suddenly struck me. 'You don't think she was making it up to get me back there, do you?' I asked anxiously.

Amy's mum stared at me, hard, and spoke very, very slowly and emphatically. 'Lainey, I most certainly do *not* think that your mother was lying. I know you don't like the choices she's made, and they certainly wouldn't suit everyone, but she's a good person and she loves you dearly. Don't even entertain that thought, OK?'

I felt quite chastened. 'OK.'

The week sped by much too fast. Amy and I did lots of makeovers, stayed up late talking, and slept late in the mornings. We visited all our old haunts, and I saw Kieran every day. It was bliss, and I realised how much I appreciated Bath now that I'd been shown a different way of life altogether. And I really, really appreciated my friends.

Kieran didn't seem at all nervous about his audition. I would have been terrified, but he told me that he'd always had a feeling that something big would happen with his music. I suppose having parents who are both famous would give you more confidence. Though maybe it was more because they encourage him so much, and are so obviously proud of him. It made me wonder what I might have been like, and whether I'd have special talents if I'd had different parents, but unfortunately we don't get to choose our family. I resigned myself to making daisy chains and drawing caricatures for the rest of my life, and I did a special one of Kieran as a good luck present. He loved it, and so did Estelle and Thomas. They even had it framed and Kieran put it in his bedroom, along with a photo that Amy took of us together. Thomas made an extra print of that for me to take back to Deepest Nottinghamshire, and I vowed to keep it in my pocket *all* the time so that no one could take it away from me.

On my last evening there we all had a party at Amy's house. We played music, and Kieran brought his guitar (Amy's mum was very impressed!), and we danced and laughed, and I tried not to think about Ivy House, and just enjoyed myself. I wanted to store up the memories so that I could bring them out and look at them every time I felt low. It was only when Amy and I went to bed, and I realised that this really was my last night in Bath, that I got weepy again. And scared. I would have given anything to not have to go back there. I made myself think of Horace, and his twitchy whiskers and snuffly rat whisper, and how happy we would both be to see each other again.

Chapter Twenty-five

Ivy House Again

Mum arrived in the car at three o'clock. She looked tired, but she gave me a huge hug, and came in for a cup of tea with Amy's mum. She didn't say anything about me running away or stealing the Community money (Amy's dad had very generously sent a cheque to Ivy House for the amount). All she said was, 'I missed you, Lainey'.

I was hoping that being in Bath, even just briefly, would make her want to move back again, but when I carefully mentioned how much happier we were here, she just shrugged and murmured that some things can't be changed. It was obvious that we really were going back there, and I felt as if a huge weight had landed on my chest and was slowly suffocating me. In a way, I'd refused to believe that I'd have to go back, and it was horrible seeing that there really was no choice.

Saying goodbye to Amy and her parents was really, really hard. Last time I left Bath I thought it was the end of the world, but at that time I'd had no idea of how truly awful it would be at Ivy House. If it wasn't for Horace reappearing I'd have run away even further, and I think Mum probably knew that and was thanking the Angel of Rats for keeping him safe and giving me a reason to return.

We drove past our old house, and it was soooo weird seeing it looking just the same, but with a different car in the driveway. I wanted to stop but Mum refused, saying that the past is the past, and best left alone.

On the way to Deepest Nottinghamshire she told me that some changes had been planned. I could sleep in a room of my own, next door to hers, away from the Crying Girl. She said that Aileen knew all about the Crying Girl, and would tell me the story if I asked her, though it's a 'very sad' story. I was also going to be allowed to take some of the vegetables out of the pans before they put the meat in, and could make myself omelettes so that I would eat more healthily. I had the distinct impression that the Community didn't like me having preferential treatment, because Mum pointed out very firmly that I really, really must make a big effort to fit in. I didn't say anything at all.

It was very late when we arrived. No one met us at the door this time, but Daisy (who looked even rounder in the tummy) and Skye came dashing over as soon as we walked in, and put their paws on my shoulders to lick my face. It was nice to see *them* again. We went straight upstairs to Mum's room and there was Horace, fast asleep in his nest. I woke him and cuddled him and cried a bit, and Horace did his rat whisper in my ear. He was very happy to see me! Then Mum showed me the little grey room next to hers, which thankfully didn't have a fireplace in it. I put Horace back in his cage and slid my bag under the bed, then we went downstairs to face the Community. Everyone but Aileen and the Small Child were rather cool with me (Aileen grinned and said hello, and the Small Child hurled herself at me as if I was her long-lost sister. It was rather endearing, actually). No one said anything about the money, which surprised me, but Bryony, Pixie, and Sparrow gave me black looks, which I ignored.

We had a cheese sandwich and I went to bed with Horace snuggled up by my feet. It was very, very quiet. No Crying Girl, which at least was something to be grateful for, I suppose. I lay awake doing some serious thinking, and realised that I had no choice but to resign myself to being stuck here. And that if I could just stay away from everyone and do my chores, I may at least be able to visit Bath sometimes. It didn't make me feel much better, but it gave me some little bright patches to look forward to.

Chapter Twenty-six

A Ghost Story

Mist was draped everywhere in the morning, lying in long strands that just allowed glimpses of the fields and trees. When I went out with Daisy and Skye to sit under 'my' tree, it looked a bit like Fairyland, only more isolated. I tried not to feel upset about being here. Instead, I let the dogs lie beside me and lean against me, and ignored the fact that my rear end was getting very damp.

I was on kitchen duty, so when I heard voices I reluctantly got to my feet and went to prepare breakfast. The first breakfast task is to get a basket and gather eggs from the hens, a job I actually like – they cluster around, clucking, when I scatter the grain, and don't seem to mind having their eggs taken away as long as one is left behind. I do wonder who it was who first saw hen's eggs and thought they'd be good to eat. My guess is that the Ancient Ones probably saw animals eating eggs and decided to give it a try.

So, I found about a dozen eggs in the coop, and took them back to the kitchen. Sarah, Aileen, and the Small Child, who I now have to call Leila all the time (another new rule) were in there already, making herbal tea. They murmured a good morning, and I surprised them by saying it back. I was Making An Effort.

Breakfast was scrambled eggs, toast, bacon, and tomatoes. I stood well back while the bacon was cooking (in a separate pan, thank goodness!) so that the smell wasn't quite as strong, and everyone else trooped down when Leila hit the gong to summon them. The Dorm Demons weren't speaking to me because I had my own room, but that was fine by me. I didn't want to talk to them anyway. Mum looked pleased to see me doing chores without complaining, and Dom complimented me on the tasty food. It eased the tension a bit.

Washing up really is hard work, because they don't use real soap here. The 'washing-up liquid' is a mixture of vinegar and baking soda, with lemon juice added to make it smell better. I loathe it because it doesn't make suds, but no 'real' cleaning products are allowed here. After I'd washed up and scrubbed the surfaces, I had to do weeding until lunchtime. Aileen had made bread, so we had that with some cheese and I went out to 'my' tree. Daisy joined me. She loves cheese (like Horace) and will practically stand on her head if she thinks that would get her a piece.

We were practicing 'sit' when Aileen strolled over and sat beside me.

'You're very good with the dogs,' she commented.

'They're nice dogs,' I said. Daisy lay down with her head in my lap. Aileen looked at her fondly.

'Well, we'll have a few more soon. Daisy's puppies are due in a week or two.'

Puppies! I couldn't help smiling at the thought, and stroked Daisy's head. 'Can I help look after them?' I asked.

Aileen grinned. 'I'll put puppy duty on your chore list.' She lay on the grass and stretched her hands above her head.

'Ellen told me you've heard the ghost,' she remarked.

So I told her about the Crying Girl, and the walls going transparent and then reappearing when I tried to help her. And Aileen recounted the story of how she came to haunt the dormitory. Here's what she told me.

A long, long time ago (hundreds of years), the Crying Girl was a servant at Ivy House (though it wasn't called Ivy House back in the old days). She was very pretty, and had an illicit relationship with the master of the house, who loved her but wasn't allowed to marry her because he was already married (and you weren't allowed to marry servants if you were high-born in those days, anyway, so he couldn't have married her even if he was single).

Then one day he went up to the servants' quarters (which is

now the dormitory), and found her with another man. He was sooooo angry that he ordered for her to be shut into the wall by the fireplace and had it all bricked in so that she would die very slowly. (That really upset me, but apparently it happened a lot in those days, especially to women). And she's been crying to be let out ever since.

The story made me shudder, and I couldn't imagine how the others could sleep in there. Aileen told me that the children have never heard her, but that when Leila was a baby, and Aileen was just getting her settled in the dorm, she heard her a few times.

'How do you know the story?' I asked.

'Because it's an old story that most people thought was just folklore, then her bones were found when the owners before us lived here. They heard her too, and had the walls excavated. She's buried in the churchyard now.'

'If she's buried, shouldn't she be at peace?'

Aileen sighed. 'Sometimes, when something very terrible has happened, it takes a long time for the memory imprint to fade. And I think your unhappiness might have been the reason why you saw and heard her.

'So if people nearby are happy, does that help?' Poor Crying Girl, stuck in those walls for hundreds of years.

'It might.' Aileen stood up and brushed grass off her dungarees, then winked at me.

For the first time since moving there, I smiled at her and she smiled back. I think I sort-of understood what she was trying to tell me.

Chapter Twenty-seven

News

Dark Matter, Kieran's band, passed the audition for *Teen Star*, and they're going to be on the show in two weeks! I walked to the phone box (miles!) and it was sooo good to hear his voice. When he told me the News, I screamed and jumped up and down! And they're playing 'my song' on the show! We couldn't talk for long, because I was only allowed to have £1 for the call, but he asked me to persuade Mum to let me stay with him that weekend, so that I could go and be in the audience to cheer for him! I jumped up and down a bit more, blew kisses down the phone (he blew lots back) and skipped all the way back to Ivy House.

I found Mum in her room, in a slightly compromising situation with Dom. Fortunately they had most of their clothes on, but they were kissing when I burst in. Yuck, how gross! Parents shouldn't be allowed to act like teenagers! They jumped apart very guiltily, and I burbled out about Kieran, and *Teen Star*, and pleaded, really pleaded, to be allowed to go that weekend.

Mum rambled on a bit about how I was trying to Make An Effort, and ended up by saying that I could go if I carried on settling in. She agreed to put me on the train to Bath on the Friday morning, and meet me off the train on the Sunday evening. But I had to promise that there would be no arguments about returning. I promised, of course.

That week I did all my chores without a murmur. I didn't interact much with the others except for Aileen, who is actually a nice person, and who told such silly stories that she made me laugh. She joined me by 'my' tree quite often, and I didn't mind her company. I even helped her to henna her hair (that's how she gets it so red). It's incredibly messy! You mix this greenish-brown powder (from the henna plant) with water until it turns into thick mud, and daub it on your hair. Then you wait for ages, and wash it out. Because I put it on for Aileen, she didn't get bits staining her face, so she was very, very pleased. If I'd had any make-up left from the Dorm Magpies, I'd have given her a makeover, but it had all gone. Mum promised to give me some money for a top when I go to *Teen Star* with Kieran, so that got me thinking about hiding places to keep it from the clutches of the ravening horde of the Dorm Demons.

The next day there was more Good News. Aileen came and woke me when it was still dark, and acted very mysterious, asking me to go with her. I put Horace in his cage, threw my clothes on, and followed her into the kitchen. There, snuggled up on a blanket in her bed, was Daisy with four tiny puppies! Skye was lying over the other side of the range, close enough to watch over them, and Daisy looked very proud of herself and thumped her tail as if to say, 'Look! Aren't I clever?' I cooed with delight and touched the puppies very gently. They were all curled up against her, suckling, and they gave funny little squeaks as they blindly clambered over each other (really they just sort of *fell* over each other, but they were *trying* to clamber!). Aileen showed me the addition to the chores list. It said 'Puppy duties – Lainey.'

When everyone else got up they made lots of fuss of Daisy and the puppies. Leila cried because she wanted to help look after them, and Bryony, Pixie, and Sparrow were quite nasty that I'd got the fun chore and made a big noise about preferential treatment. I chose Leila as my helper, because there's a lot of cleaning up to do with puppies around, and she's the only one who's nice to me. Maybe it's because she's only little, and hasn't learned to be influenced by others yet.

I wrote long letters to Kieran and Amy, telling them that I was allowed to stay at Kieran's, and all about the puppies. I wished I still had my camera-phone so that I could send pictures of them, but of course that had disappeared along with everything else I owned.

That night I didn't get much sleep. I kept getting up to check that Daisy and the puppies were OK. Daisy and Skye didn't seem to mind, especially when I gave them both a piece of cheese as a new mum and dad present.

Chapter Twenty-eight

Back to Bath

I was so busy with the puppies and the chores that the days passed very quickly. Apart from Aileen and Leila, who was actually quite sweet for a Small Child, and helped more than I'd expected, I hardly saw the others except at meals. That suited me fine. Mum was like a stranger. Even though she was in the bedroom next to mine I only saw her with everyone else at mealtimes, and the rest of the time she was either doing chores or disappearing off with Dom. They seemed to have quite a 'thing' going, which I found vaguely nauseating. Dom was friendly towards me, but not pushy, which was easier to deal with than being around Creepy Lincoln, who I was being very, very careful to avoid.

The puppies were gorgeous! I fell in love with all of them, but was completely besotted by the smallest one (the runt, Aileen said), a female with a dark grey coat that was fluffier than the others. I called her Molly, and she had the funniest little face that always made her look as if she was smiling. The others (Leila and I decided) were Polly, Nelly, and Buttercup (Leila chose Buttercup's name, and it was a bit unfortunate because he's a boy puppy!). Aileen told me that at least one of the puppies was going to a local farmer to be a hunting dog, but that they'd stay with us until they were nine weeks old, to learn doggie socialising skills and get properly weaned. I hoped Molly would be staying at Ivy House.

Mum finally emerged the day before my trip to Bath, and took me into town for two T-shirts, a pair of jeans, and some pumps. Shopping was heaven! I've always loved shopping, but I appreciated that trip more than anything, because there weren't any shops to wander round nearby so it felt even more like a huge treat. We had lunch at a restaurant that did really nice Italian food, and I had the most amazing pasta in creamy cheese sauce, and salad with feta and olives, and ice cream. We actually called a truce enough to have a conversation over lunch, though I still resented her for forcing me to live at Ivy House. She told me that she and Dom were An Item (as if I hadn't already known), and that they were setting up a business together. That made me curious.

'What sort of business?'

Mum leaned forward and her eyes shone. I have to admit that she looks happier than I've seen her since she caught Dad being a love rat.

'Dom's brilliant at metalwork, and we're designing and making jewellery and mobiles out of recycled cutlery.'

I was puzzled. 'You mean old knives and forks?'

'Yes. And spoons, too. I'll show you some when you get back.'

'It sounds weird.'

Mum laughed. 'It actually looks really good. Just wait, and you'll see.'

Maybe she thought it would tempt me back like the amazing discovery of Horace in the fireplace had, but it didn't have the same appeal at all. Thinking of Horace got me worried about whether anyone would let him out while I was away, but Mum promised to keep him in her room and look after him.

The last shop we went in was at my insistence, even though Mum didn't approve. I came out with a small canvas travel-bag and two padlocks. In case you're thinking I planned to lock my things up on the trip back home, I wasn't using that bag for the journey. This was my Cunning Plan to protect the last of my belongings from the Ravening Hordes. I put my special things in the bag, padlocked the zip, then padlocked the bag handles to the bottom of my bed. Hah! I was back to being resourceful again!

Friday morning, early, we drove to the station. I jumped in the car a lot more enthusiastically than on the journeys to Ivy

House, and Mum said she would phone Kieran's house that evening to make sure I'd arrived safely. Then I was on the train, whooshing through the countryside, each second taking me closer to Bath, and Kieran, and Amy, and *Teen Star*!

Kieran met me at Bath Spa station and gave me the biggest hug *ever*. We walked to his house all wrapped around each other and talked at top speed. He was feeling a little bit nervous about the show, but said that would help his performance. I would have been terrified! I told him all about the puppies, and how I hoped Molly would stay. And I showed him the photo he'd given me, which was in my pocket as always, but looking a bit battered and crumpled now. He laughed and promised to get Estelle to take lots more pics over the weekend.

Estelle and Thomas were very welcoming, as always, and Estelle gave me a motherly hug. I wish she was my mother, and told her so, which made her a bit teary-eyed. She's the coolest mother I've ever met. Amy came round and we had a feast, although Estelle didn't eat much. She said making all the food made her feel full-up already, and she was impressed by my kitchen duties but refused to let me wash the dishes, even though they have real washing-up liquid as well as a dishwasher.

Mum phoned and spoke to Estelle, who assured her that I was safe and sound. We went to Kieran's room and talked, and played music, and talked some more, and laughed a lot. Then Amy left, making us promise to call her after the show (she really wanted to go, but she was watching it live on TV), and Kieran and I snuggled up, which made me feel very warm inside, until Estelle tapped on the door and reminded us that we had an early start in the morning.

My bedroom was all white, with a pink duvet and sheets and a pink fluffy throw. There was a hairdryer on the dressing table, and some Chanel make-up with a little note beside it that said 'Use me,' which made me feel as if I was in a fairy tale. And the room had an en-suite shower room – sheer bliss! I stood under the shower for ages, feeling Ivy House wash out of my pores. Estelle had left a glass and a jug of water by the bed, too. She is soooo thoughtful and kind. I wanted to lie awake holding all the best moments of the day in my mind, but was asleep within moments of curling up in the beautiful soft bed.

Chapter Twenty-nine

Teen Star

It felt soooo nice waking up in Kieran's house, in my beautiful room. As I was coming to, I was just about to leap up to see to the puppies when I remembered that I was in Bath, and so I lay and stretched luxuriously and stroked the fluffy throw instead. After a while I heard someone moving around, so I jumped in the shower and washed my hair, then dried it and put on some make-up (it was lush, Estelle had obviously chosen it with my colouring in mind), checked myself in the tall mirror, and went downstairs.

Estelle and Thomas were in the kitchen, popping toast out of the toaster and taking chocolate croissants from the oven. They both gave me big smiles and told me to sit down in the dining room and pour myself some tea or coffee to go with my orange juice. Kieran came in moments later, still damp from the shower, and sat beside me to give me a quick, surreptitious kiss. He smelled of herbal shampoo and soap, and his hair hung in long wet spirals. I couldn't resist taking a strand and pulling it straight, just to watch it bounce back. It was so surreal to be at Kieran's house that I felt like pinching myself in case I was dreaming!

We all took the train to Paddington Station because it was quicker than driving, and a car with a chauffeur met us at the station! We knew it was for us because the driver was holding up a placard that said, 'Kieran Kamau'. I felt like a movie star, and a few people looked at us as if they thought we might be, too!

Kieran was whisked away as soon as we arrived, to get together with the rest of the band and go into make-up. When

Estelle, Thomas, and I sat down in the front of the audience we were all so excited and nervous that we kept fidgeting. Well, Estelle and I did. Thomas seemed very calm. Maybe Kieran gets his lack of nerves from his dad. I looked around to see where the cameras were, and hoped that everyone we knew was watching and would vote for Dark Matter.

The lights dimmed eventually, and Tony Carr, the host, walked onto the stage. Everyone clapped and whistled, and after a minute he raised his hands to calm us all down, then chatted for a while about the great acts that were coming. He's taller than he looks on television, and thinner. Estelle whispered to me that the cameras add a few pounds, which explained it. Then Tony introduced the first act, a girl band. They were very good (and braver than me to even go up there!). Then it was a boy, who sang a really lovely romantic song that made me feel quite slushy. That made me nervous in case everyone voted for him. Then another two bands – by then I was so nervous that I couldn't concentrate, and I glanced at Estelle, who looked nervous too, and at Thomas, who looked very calm. I wondered how Kieran and the rest of the band were feeling.

Finally, *finally*, Dark Matter was announced, the last act! They strolled onto the stage as if they owned it. Kieran stood right at the front with his guitar, looked straight at us, smiled, and launched into the opening bars of the song. I almost *died* with excitement! I'd heard the song quite a few times, of course, but never with the whole band playing it – Kieran had told me they sent files backwards and forwards over the internet to get all the instruments right. It sounded amazing, and Kieran's voice sent shivers up my spine. I quickly glanced around at the rest of the audience, and they looked spellbound.

When the last notes died away the audience burst into applause, even more than for the other acts. People stood to clap, and we did, too. It was obvious that the TV audience loved Dark Matter best!

After they left the stage, Tony Carr came back and said that the whole country was already voting. He showed clips from each act (I was very glad that Thomas had set the DVD player to record the show), then talked a bit, and told some jokes, while the tension in the studio got higher and higher.

Finally, when I thought I'd expire from nerves, he announced the winner. It was Dark Matter! I screamed (I think Estelle did, too), and there was huge applause as the band came back onstage to shake hands with Tony Carr, who asked Kieran whether he had anything to say. Kieran grinned at him, then turned to face the audience and cameras. 'Thank you to our families and friends, to everyone here, and to everyone who voted for us. I can't begin to tell you how much this means to us. And a special thank you to Lainey for inspiring the song.' He looked right at me as he said it, and the cameras turned to focus on me, too. I smiled at Kieran and blew him a kiss. Tony Carr shook hands with them all again (the band members looked ecstatic), and wrapped up the show after they walked off.

The boys had to do an interview with the press afterwards, which took ages. The other parents waited with us, and everyone was ablaze with excitement. Then we all went out for dinner in a huge crowd, and had champagne (I was allowed some too!) and I kept saying 'You won!' Kieran kissed me over and over, and we phoned Amy from his mobile, and cameras kept flashing, and it was the best night of my entire life! I really, really thought I would explode with happiness!

Chapter Thirty

Rising Star

It was very, very late when we arrived back at Kieran's house. Their answerphone was winking with about a million messages – lots from family and friends, and loads and loads from the press. Newspapers and TV wanted to interview him, and they'd only won that heat, not the entire show! The Final was still five weeks away! It seemed that Kieran had something that people thought was very special. Well, I thought so too, of course!

Estelle, Thomas, and Kieran spoke to people they knew after we'd had some sleep, and a few more press people rang in the morning. It meant I hardly spoke to Kieran, because he was so busy talking to people, and my train was at two o'clock, but he smiled at me a lot, and Amy came round so that we could say goodbye to each other properly.

Just before we left for the train station Kieran took me aside. He kissed me and looked deep into my eyes in a way that made me go all shivery. 'I'll come and visit you in a couple of weeks, OK?' he said.

'At Ivy House?' I was stunned!

'Well, your mum won't be too thrilled if you come here too often, and I want to see you before the Final. You'll come down for the Final though, won't you?' He looked quite anxious, so I told him that nothing, not floods or fire or crazy mums would keep me from being there.

It was very sad saying goodbye to Estelle and Robert. I hugged them both, and they told me I was welcome anytime. When Kieran, Amy, and I left the house there were people outside, who took photos of us and called out questions to Kieran. He good-naturedly waved at them and said he was delighted they'd been chosen, and was taking his girlfriend to catch her train. So they took photos of both of us together, and with Amy. We all felt very special and important, and I was glad that I was having a Good Hair Day that day!

At the station a couple of girls came over to us and congratulated Kieran. They flirted a bit with him, but he kept his arm around me and kissed me when the train rolled into the station.

'I'm going to miss you, Lainey,' he whispered. I tried very, very hard not to cry.

'I'll miss you too,' I said, sniffing a bit.

Amy and I hugged, then Kieran kissed me again and they stood watching as I got onto the train. He blew me a kiss. 'See you in two weeks in Deepest Nottinghamshire,' he called. That made me smile, and I was still smiling as the train moved away, leaving them behind.

Chapter Thirty-one

Ivy House, Again

Mum and Dom's weird jewellery is actually quite clever, I have to admit. I was sort-of expecting it to be entire knives and forks dangling from earrings and necklaces, which would be not only weird but also very sharp and heavy! But it isn't, thank goodness. Dom has lots of tools, and they'd cut the pieces of cutlery up then twisted them into all sorts of interesting shapes. The mobiles were big, and made tinkling noises, but the jewellery quite dainty. Mum told me that a few shops were already interested in selling them, and one (wow!) is in Bath! I got all hopeful that she might want to move back there, but she said they would have to be selling a *lot* before that would even be vaguely possible.

My padlocks worked, so I put my Chanel make-up from Estelle, and my new clothes, in the bag. Horace was delighted to see me – he snuffled like mad in my ear, and ran up and down both of my arms in a little rat dance. And the puppies had grown a bit in just two days!

We had to ask the Community for permission for Kieran to come and stay. Sarah griped a bit until Mum said that she would pay extra for his room that weekend (thank goodness he wouldn't be in with the Dorm Demons and the Crying Girl!). After money was mentioned there was a unanimous agreement, so I walked to the phone box to let Kieran know. His phone was engaged, so although I was a bit disappointed not to speak to him, I left a message to say it was all arranged, and asked him to write to tell me what time his train was arriving.

Buttercup and Nelly had been chosen as hunting dogs by the farmer. I was relieved that he hadn't chosen Molly, who squirmed and kissed my face when I picked her up. Then it was back to the chores.

Pixie came over as I was churning milk, and I looked up in surprise. She usually avoided me. She stood right in front on me and put her hands on her hips.

'Well, Little Miss Privilege,' she started. I stared at her. 'You really think you're something, don't you?'

I shrugged and carried on churning. It was hard work.

Pixie ticked off her fingers, one by one. 'A room of your own. Trips away. A boy coming to stay. Puppy duties. You're nothing but a sneaky thief, and you get all the best treatment. Watch your back, that's all I have to say to you.'

She turned to walk away. I knew, really *knew* that I should stay calm and not say one word. But before she'd gone five steps my mouth had opened of its own accord.

'If you weren't so horrible to me, I wouldn't have run away. And the money came back, so you didn't lose anything. You stole *my* things. Just leave me alone, you bully!'

Of course, as soon as the words slipped out, I knew I had made a Terrible Mistake. Pixie turned around, and the look she gave me was far, far worse than Dianne's Killer Glare or my disdainful lip-lift. It was sheer, unadulterated, undiluted hatred, and I actually felt quite scared. She took two steps towards me with her fists clenched in front of her, and I stepped backwards. Then she stopped, gave a nasty sneering smile, and stalked away.

I carried on churning. My insides churned along with the rapidly curdling milk.

That night, when I went to bed, my bag had been slashed apart. All my things were missing. Mum found my T-shirts the next day, trampled into some cowpats, but there was no sign of my lovely Chanel make-up. Even Mum looked upset. She asked for a Conference at lunchtime, but Sarah, Tink, and Creepy Lincoln refused, saying that issues between the children had to be sorted out by the children. Aileen tried to intervene and was told to step out of it.

So much for trying to settle in.

Chapter Thirty-two

Kieran

The next two weeks were a nightmare. Pixie, Bryony, and Sparrow ganged up at every opportunity, always waiting until I was alone before appearing with snide remarks and threats. I used the padlocks from my wrecked bag to lock my door with, because I was terrified that something bad would happen to Horace. Of course, I should have thought of locking my door before, but it's Forbidden in the Community. I'd really had enough of their Rules by then, because different Rules seemed to apply to different members.

The days dragged by, and I did my best to avoid everyone. Finally, *finally* the day came when Mum drove me to meet Kieran at the station. I have never, ever been so happy to see anyone in my whole life! He stepped off the train with a small bag and his guitar in a soft case slung over his shoulder and a huge smile on his face, and I ran and *threw* myself at him, almost knocking him over – a bit like Daisy and Skye when visitors arrive. He gave me a bear hug, swung me round, and said hello very politely to Mum. And he exclaimed over the countryside as we drove back to Ivy House, saying how lovely it was around here. I found it hard to conceive of it as lovely, considering it was my prison, but looking at it through the BOMDs eyes did give the area a bit of a glow.

Everyone was in the kitchen, and the puppies were running around getting under our feet. Daisy and Skye did their big welcome act, putting their paws on Kieran's shoulders, and he made a fuss of them both. The adults greeted Kieran in a friendly manner, Sparrow sniffed and walked out, and Pixie and Bryony stared and stared at him as if they couldn't believe their eyes. Well, he *is* gorgeous! Pixie moved over to make space for him beside her, but not enough space for me too, so I took his arm and steered him over the other side of the table where we could sit together. I had vegetables for dinner, while they had rabbit stew (Skye was doing the hunting while Daisy was busy with her babies), and I sniggered a bit at Kieran's surprised expression when he looked at his plate, but he ate it without saying a word.

Of course, no one at Ivy House watches television or reads newspapers, so they'd never heard of *Teen Star*, but they were interested in Kieran's guitar and asked him to play after the clearing up had been done. Creepy Lincoln fetched a hand drum, Tink dug out a mandolin, and Sarah banged away on a bodhran (an Irish drum – she was very out of rhythm, even I noticed, but Kieran didn't mention it, he just kept on playing). Pixie and Bryony gazed adoringly at Kieran, and kept telling him how brilliant he was, which got me very worried that they were going to try to steal him away.

It turned out that my worries had some foundation. All weekend it was hard to get any time alone with Kieran at all. Wherever we went, Pixie would pop up like a rabbit out of a hole, or Bryony would suddenly appear and join us. My stolen make-up was much in evidence, and I refrained from mentioning that mascara goes on your eyelashes and not in puddles over your eyes. They ignored me completely, of course, and flirted outrageously with him. The happy, romantic weekend that I'd been so looking forward to took on a nightmarish quality, but Kieran laughed when I mentioned that it would be nice to be on our own for a while, and said they were just being friendly. Well, they were friendly to *him*!

I thought that the lowest moment was when we were just getting into kissing under 'my' tree and Bryony strolled across like a demon stalker and sat down with us. But no, worse was to come. When I passed his bedroom that night, intending to creep in and get a few minutes alone with him, I heard voices from inside. I opened the door and there was Pixie, on his bed, lying all stretched out in what she clearly thought was a seductive pose, while Kieran stood near the door looking a bit uncomfortable and embarrassed. Of course, I should have gone in there and made myself at home, but I stupidly stormed out and then tortured myself all night, wondering whether he liked her better than me.

By the time Mum drove us back to the station on Sunday, the atmosphere between Kieran and I was a little tense. Mum wandered off a bit to give us time alone, which was very tactful of her, considering our lack of privacy at Ivy House, and Kieran pulled me over to sit on a bench with him. He stroked my hair away from my face (I'd been hiding behind it most of the weekend), and looked directly in my eyes.

'I'm sorry it wasn't a very nice weekend,' I told him miserably.

Kieran smiled. 'I can see why those girls drive you nuts,' he said. My spirits lifted a bit.

'Really? I thought you liked them.'

'They were just trying to wind you up. Ignore them, OK? It's you that I love, Lainey.'

My heart gave a huge bump. I looked at Kieran. He looked back at me.

'Did you say you love me?' I hardly dared check, in case I'd misheard and he laughed at me. Kieran kissed me on the nose, then my eyelids, then my mouth.

'Yes,' he said.

The train arrived before I could even think of anything to say, and Kieran jumped up and picked up his bag and guitar. 'Promise you'll come to the Final in three weeks. I really need you there, Lainey!' he almost shouted over the noise of the loudspeaker system announcing the train. I nodded. The train stopped and doors opened. Kieran clambered on and stood in the doorway. Mum wandered over to stand beside me and called goodbye. The doors closed, and Kieran pulled the window down and peeked out.

'Bye! I love you!' he shouted.

I jumped up and down, waving and shouting back.

'I love you too!' I yelled. I could feel Mum looking at me but I didn't care. I waved until the train went round the corner, even though he couldn't see us any more.

On the drive home, Mum was quiet. As we pulled into the parking area at Ivy House and the car stopped, she turned and looked at me.

'I can see why you like him,' was all she said.

I went straight to my room and hugged myself tightly. My mind was like a loop tape, spinning the words round and round. Kieran loves me. Kieran loves me. Eventually the rhythm of the words sent me to sleep.

Chapter Thirty-three

Home Sweet Home (Not)

For just over two weeks, life went on much as before at Ivy House. Sarah bossed everyone around. Tink disappeared in between Chores to do what he did best (tinkering), and put together a hand-plough from some old bits and pieces (it did actually work, which was quite impressive). Creepy Lincoln crept around. Aileen was her usual sunny-natured self, singing while she did her Chores, praising me for how well the puppies were doing (though the credit for that was Daisy's, not mine), and joining me under 'my' tree sometimes. She liked Kieran a lot, and said that he was lucky to have me as his girlfriend. I even confided that we loved each other in a moment of warm camaraderie. The Dorm Demons were as vile as ever, but at least they hadn't been able to get into my room since the incident of the wrecked bag – not that there was anything much in there apart from Horace now. Little Leila was so sweet that I became very fond of her, and hoped that she wouldn't absorb the Evil Vibrations by osmosis from the others through sharing the dorm with them.

Mum was hardly ever around. Her Chores always seemed to be at the opposite end of the Community, and she spent most of her free time with Dom, creating the weird cutlery stuff. The one evening that we did do the washing up together she told me that they had lots of orders, especially for the jewellery, and that it was starting to bring in quite a good income. That gave me Hope of Escape, but she brushed the idea off when I mentioned it. Mum seemed to be living in a different world to me.

This was brought home to me even more harshly when I came across Creepy Lincoln in the corridor on my way up to my room. I turned the corner and there he was, leering at me. I stepped sideways to avoid him, and he moved in the same direction. I side-stepped again and he matched my steps, blocking me from going forward. My heart raced faster and faster and I felt dizzy with panic. Creepy Lincoln laughed. 'Kiss me and I'll let you past,' he said. I walked backwards, touching the wall to keep my balance, and he moved towards me like one of the cats stalking a mouse, grinning like a demon in a horror movie.

'If you touch me I'll scream,' I shouted. He leaned forward and I could smell rotting teeth on his breath.

'You're free enough with that boyfriend of yours,' he hissed.

Just as I opened my mouth to scream, I heard footsteps and turned to see Sarah coming up behind me. It's the only time I've ever felt relieved to see her. She gave me a dirty look as she squeezed past and I took the opportunity to run to my room, bumping into both of them, and ignored her outraged yells to come back and apologise. Once there, I slammed the door shut, pulled my bed in front of it to stop anyone getting in, and sat down clutching my stomach. I felt sick with disgust and horror.

There seemed to be no point in telling Mum. No one would believe me. I felt hopelessly, terrifyingly alone, and Bath seemed a universe away.

The next day I avoided everyone. A letter arrived from Amy so, accompanied by Skye, I took it to 'my' tree, opening the envelope as I walked, and started reading it still standing up. In it was such a huge surprise that I had to sit down rather quickly. Amy had given up on the suave urban charms of John Carter, who she decided had all the makings of a love rat (Hooray! It took her a year, but she saw through him eventually!). She was going out with Scotty, who she said was no longer spotty and was actually quite lush, and who had won her over with his sweet stammery shyness and utter devotion. She was just beginning to realise that she liked him when Dianne let slip a comment that he *did* only blush when she was around, so she made the first move and asked him out! That shocked me even more than the fact that they were now an item!

Well. I was really, *really* pleased for Amy and for Scotty. Then I felt upset and left out. It made me miss them all terribly, and it seemed as if I was stuck out here in the Dark Ages while my friends all had normal lives. I hugged Skye, who was very comforting, and sniffled a bit to myself until a shadow loomed over me and made me jump. I looked up, expecting it to be Aileen. But it was the Dorm Demons, all three of them, looking very, very mean and nasty.

Chapter Thirty-four

The Dorm Demons' Revenge

My heart sank all the way to my feet. I started to stuff the letter into the side pocket of my jeans, but Pixie grabbed my arm and Bryony tore the letter off me. She danced away with it, reading bits out aloud in a silly voice while Pixie and Sparrow laughed.

'Give me that! It's mine,' I shouted, jumping to my feet to grapple with Bryony. Sparrow pushed me away so hard that I fell over and wrenched my knee. Tears sprang to my eyes and I blinked hard. I didn't want them to see how upset I was. Slowly and carefully Bryony tore the letter into tiny pieces and flung them in the air. Bits of paper blew across the field.

'You are the most vile, loathsome people I have *ever* met!' I screamed.

Then it got much, much worse.

Grinning, Pixie took another letter out of her pocket and waved it in front of me. The envelope had Kieran's handwriting on it, and it had been opened. I leaped forward, squeaking with pain as my knee gave out. 'You thief! That's for me!'

'How do you know, Little Miss Privilege?' she jeered, taking out the letter and wafting it just out of reach. 'It could be for me. Then again, it could be for you, telling you he's dumped you.'

I reached out, trying to sound calm (I'd read somewhere that's the best approach when dealing with psychopaths). 'Pixie, that's enough. Give it to me. Please.'

Pixie did her Evil Grin again, and Sparrow and Bryony each took one of my arms as I struggled to get free. She pulled out the letter. 'Dreary Lainey, you are so boring that I can't stand the sight of you any more. You're dumped. Kieran.' She intoned.

'You're making it up,' I yelled. Most of me knew she must be lying but another part of me (the scared, low-confidence part) almost believed it was true. After all, why would gorgeous BOMD Kieran, who was going to be famous, want to be around me, the girl with the now permanent BHD, buried in the countryside, hours away?

They all laughed as Pixie tore that letter up too, and pieces wafted away like snow. Then I understood what it means to 'see red' because I really, really did see a red mist everywhere. I have never, in my whole life, been so angry.

I pretended to slump, which they sort-of expected. After all, they'd defeated and humiliated me. Then I jabbed my elbow into Sparrow's unmentionable bits and heard him groan as he buckled over and fell on the ground, gasping. Now that arm was free I swung it around, hard, and punched Bryony in the face. She staggered a bit and my other arm was free. Then I ran as fast as I could, limping so that my gait was all lopsided, back to the house, and burst in the kitchen as if the Hounds of Hell were after me (though I'm sure they wouldn't be as bad as the Dorm Demons).

Unfortunately for me, Sarah was on cooking duty that day, and she whirled around as I practically fell through the door, swiftly pursued by Pixie.

'What the …?' she cried.

Before I could catch my breath to speak, Pixie did a massive Drama Queen act, telling Sarah that I'd attacked Sparrow and Bryony when they were trying to be friendly, and that they both needed help. Not stopping to listen to any explanation from me, Sarah dashed out of the door, Pixie leading the way to the Wounded Heroes.

I was banished to my room while a House Conference was held without me. Afterwards Mum came and tapped on my door. Sparrow had recovered, but Bryony's nose was swollen. 'Good, I said, 'That'll teach her to keep it out of other people's business!' Mum sighed and sat on my bed.

'Lainey, I don't understand why you're being so hostile,' she murmured.

I explained about the letters, and showed Mum the remains of my bag. She looked sad, but told me that a decision had been made, and she couldn't go against the Community Rules.

'But I wasn't there to tell the truth! They all lied,' I raged.

'The point is, Lainey, you injured two residents.' Mum seemed as deaf as everyone else.

The decision was that I was grounded in my room for a whole *week*. Even my meals would be brought here. A very, very awful thought struck me.

'It's the *Teen Star* Final in just under a week, Mum! I *have* to go, I *promised* Kieran I'd be there!'

Mum shook her head and stood up. 'Sorry, Lainey. No trip to Bath or London, or anywhere else for that matter. No phone calls. No letters. No privileges at all.'

I grabbed her hand, trying to ignore Niagara Falls trying to escape from my eyes. 'Please Mum! Don't do this to me!'

Mum stood up, shaking her head, and walked to the door. Then she came back and held out her hand.

'What?' I asked.

'The key to your door padlock, please.'

'No!'

'Lainey, the key.'

I gave it to her. Mum left, and I heard the padlock click into place. As her footsteps moved further away, I screamed, 'I hate this place! And I hate you!'

I had never, ever felt so horribly alone.

Chapter Thirty-five

Running Away. Again

It really was like being in prison. The Community clearly thought that Mum might be tempted to be too soft on me, so my meals were brought by Sarah, who refused to speak to me or listen to my pleas. I paced the room for hours. I wept. I cuddled Horace, who snuffled sympathetically in my ear. I worried about Kieran not hearing from me. And about that letter from him. And about Amy, who'd be wondering why she hadn't had a reply to her letter.

On the third day, two days from the *Teen Star* Final, I looked at the small window and wondered whether I could (a) squeeze through it and (b) *if* that was possible, whether I'd break my legs or my neck climbing down to the ground. I decided to take the risk.

I waited until after Sarah had taken away my dinner plate and it was dark outside. The house was so big that I couldn't hear anyone anyway, but I hoped they'd all be indoors by now. The bed was heavy and squeaked across the floor when I dragged it across to the window, and I waited, holding my breath, but no one came. The window was awfully small but I pushed it as far open as it would go, and stuck my head and shoulders through the gap. It was a very, very tight squeeze, but my body followed as I turned and wriggled onto the ledge outside. Then I looked down, and rather wished I hadn't. It was a long, long way to the ground, and the only things to hold were a pipe and lots of ivy. I took a deep breath and grasped the pipe with one hand and a thick trunk of ivy with the other.

'Tarzan, Superman, Spiderman, and all you other heroes, where are you when I need you?' I muttered under my breath.

No one appeared. It took ages to slowly move down, one hand hold at a time, but after an eternity I reached solid ground. I was shaking all over.

The next part of The Plan, getting to Bath, posed a bit of a problem because I had no money, and creeping into the kitchen to find the money tin wasn't an option. I walked to the phone box, leaping into the hedges every time I heard a car coming, and dialled the operator to ask for a reverse charge call to Kieran. She put me through, and the phone was engaged.

'Please keep trying. It's an emergency,' I begged. The phone stayed engaged. I gave her Amy's number instead and, thankfully, Amy's mother answered. She was going to turn down the call when the operator let me say it was me, so she took it.

'Lainey, whatever is wrong?' she asked.

I explained about the letters, and the imprisonment, and not being able to get through to Kieran, and *Teen Star*, sobbing so much that she could hardly understand me. Amy's mum said that she'd ask Amy (who was out with Scotty) to contact Kieran and let him know.

'No, I have to be there! I need to get to Bath! I'm going to hitch a ride,' I sniffled.

There was a shocked silence for just a moment. Amy's mum's voice was very, very firm. 'Lainey, you must *not* hitchhike! It's dangerous, and foolish. Go back home, and I'll pass on your message.'

'I can't go back there!' By then I was almost hysterical. The headlights of a car swerved round the corner and the car pulled up right next to me. I turned to see Sarah getting out, and shrank further into the call box. 'Sarah's caught me,' I yelled. 'Please, please get me away from here!'

Sarah reached into the call box, grabbed my arm in a vice-like grip, and disconnected the phone as she pulled me out.

'You. Are. In. Very. Deep. Trouble.' She hissed as she pushed me into the car.

I was. I got an extra day in prison for trying to escape, and my window was nailed shut. Then The Letter came.

Chapter Thirty-six

A Letter From Amy

Hey Lainey,

Mum told me you rang, and said you're having a really, really awful time. It sounds like something out of a horror flick there, and when I'm a real scientist I'll concoct some chemical to make the Dorm Demons turn green and grow scales. I have a cunning plan for your escape, though!! The parents have agreed to come (with me too!) and fetch you the day after tomorrow – you can stay for as long as you need to. We made a deal over it. I've promised to wash up <u>every single day</u>, and do <u>all</u> the housework, and I volunteered your help, hehe! ☺

I told Kieran that you were in prison, and he was really upset and wanted to come and fetch you <u>IMMEDIATELY</u>, but he had rehearsals with the band, and couldn't. He was <u>devastated</u> that you couldn't be there.

Now, <u>Teen Star</u>. I'll put you out of your misery straight away. I won't torture you by procrastinating, hehe!!! <u>DARK MATTER WON</u>!!!!!!!!!!!!!!!!!!!!!! ☺ ☺ ☺ ☺ *It's been all over the TV and the papers, and they're on YouTube. They got lots of money, and a recording contract with Vroom! Kieran is <u>sooooo</u> famous already, and is being interviewed <u>all</u> the time, and chauffeured around in limousines, and is now a <u>VIP</u>! Yay!! When they won, he said that he wished his girlfriend could have been there to celebrate with him, and you could see all the girls in the audience going all glittery-eyed. He looooves you, Lainey.* ☺

As for me. Well, it's not been the same here without you. I miss you soooo much, and can't wait to see you! I'm still going out with Scotty – actually, I really, really like him, which is kind of strange after not even noticing him for so long.

We have loads and loads to catch up on! See you in two days! You should get this letter before then, if the Dorm Demons haven't got to it first!

Luv
Amy
XXX

Fortunately, Mum collected the post so I did get the letter. I took it to my room and read it fast, then slowly, then fast again, and leaped in the air, cheering. I looked at the date on the letter. Two days ago. They were coming that day! I decided not to say anything to anyone, in case they locked me in a cellar or something. At least once Amy's parents (oh how I loved them in that moment!) arrived with Amy, the Community would have to let me go.

I had a shower, washed my hair, and put on my clean jeans (I only had two pairs now, after the Dorm Demons had filched my stuff) and a T-shirt. Then I carried on with my Chores (I was on kitchen duty, which was very good luck as it meant I'd hear the car coming up the drive), and played with the puppies in between. They were nearly old enough to go to their new home now, and lolloped about all over the place, getting underfoot and being very cute. I wished I could take Molly with me. She was the most adorable puppy I'd ever seen, so affectionate and funny.

Just as I was dishing up dinner (rabbit again, prepared by Tink, and vegetables cooked by me), I heard a car pull up outside and dashed out. It was them! I screamed and ran just as Amy swung the back door open and leaped out. She screamed too, and we hugged each other. Her parents got out more sedately, and Amy's mum gave me a hug. I could hardly believe I was escaping, even temporarily, and I was so happy that I cried. Amy's mum patted my arm and asked to speak to my mum. The adults went into the kitchen, where the Community were about to start eating, and asked Mum for a

120

private word. They went into the front living room. Amy and I, arms tightly linked, crept under the window to listen.

We could only hear bits of the conversation because they were all talking quietly, but it sounded as if Amy's parents (oh *how* I loved them!!) were having Very Strong Words with Mum about what had been going on in the Community. Mum protested a bit that I had refused to settle in, but Amy's mum (whose voice rose at that point, so we heard her clearly) said that this was a Very Cruel Situation to put me in, that there seemed to be no ethics at Ivy House, and that she should seriously reconsider her priorities. I felt like applauding, and gave a little squeak, but Amy put her hand over my mouth.

They left the room just after that, and Amy and I went up to my room. She was stunned at how small and bare and grey it was. I put what was left of my belongings into the ripped bag, and picked up Horace's cage. No way was I leaving him here!

'It really is like a prison,' Amy whispered.

I showed her the dormitory and the wall where the Crying Girl was, and she shuddered. We quickly made our way downstairs.

Amy's parents were already in the car, waiting for us. We put Horace's cage in between us on the back seat, threw my ripped bag in the boot (my clothes kept falling out of it), and drove away. I didn't say goodbye to Mum, even though she stood in the doorway, crying a bit, and I didn't look back, not even once.

Chapter Thirty-seven

Big Changes

We stopped for a meal at a café along the motorway, then sped onwards to Bath. Amy's parents were very, very kind to me, and said that I could stay as long as I liked, and Amy's mum took my clothes out of the ripped bag and ceremoniously dumped it in the bin, saying that it belonged to the past now. I wept with relief, embarrassed that I seemed to cry *soooo* much nowadays. Amy joked that now we really were like sisters, and we caught up on lots of news on the way home, though she saved the details of her relationship with Scotty until we were snuggled up in our beds with mugs of hot chocolate and a packet of biscuits. I was astonished that she'd had the courage to ask him out! Amy told me she had surprised herself, too, but that it was easier because she knew, just *knew*, that he would say 'yes'. Apparently Scotty had gone soooo red that he looked like a tomato, then stammered that he would be honoured to be her boyfriend! It took a few days before he stopped blushing every time they met up.

As you know, Amy used to spend a lot of time at my house, because her parents work such long hours. They'd both taken the day off to fetch me (what amazing people!), and Amy's mum explained that both of us would be in charge, and that she had arranged for me to go back to school. I could hardly *believe* that I would be happy at the thought of school, but I was, and I swore to work hard and Fulfil My Potential, because I wanted Amy's parents to feel that they had made the right decision by having me there.

The days flew by. Determined to make them glad to have me around, I worked hard at school, did lots of Chores (which didn't feel like Chores here), and offered to help cook the meals, and made myself soooo useful that Amy's dad said they should employ me as their house organiser, and gave me an allowance!

As for Kieran, well, I thought he would be delighted that I was back in Bath, but I didn't see much of him. He phoned and came round the day after we got home, and was as lovely as ever when we went to the park on our own for a while. But something had changed. His life was filled with Dark Matter, and recording studios, and press interviews, and they'd already been booked to do lots of gigs. We agreed to meet during school breaks, but of course he was in the year above me, so we had to rush to get together as soon as the bell rang, and somehow other people were always crowding around him, wanting to talk to him, too. Kieran was the school hero and its new claim to fame, and even the teachers were proud of him. It seemed that suddenly he wasn't mine any more – he belonged to the whole city.

Another big change was the girls. Kieran was swamped by admirers, all flirting with him, and inviting him to parties, and Amy had to remind me that Kieran was my boyfriend, not theirs, when I got jealous and sulked. Being sensible, she also reminded me that sulking was very unappealing, and that the way to keep Kieran's love was to be happy around him – which I was in the rare moments when we were alone.

Cameras seemed to be focused on Kieran everywhere, and often on me, too. His smiling face was on the cover of *Luscious*, a gossip magazine, and there was a picture inside of both of us kissing in the park that we had no idea had been taken. I would be walking to school with Amy, when suddenly someone would jump out from a shop doorway and take snaps of me, asking how things were with Kieran and I. It was very disconcerting, especially as they always seemed to take pics of me on a BHD or when I looked extra scruffy and uncool.

When Amy was out with Scotty, I saw Dianne and Hannah and Rosa (who were all very envious of my relationship with Kieran, but were nice about it). And I visited Estelle a lot. She still felt like the mum of my dreams, and she was a little concerned that fame was taking Kieran away from the nest too early. We confided a lot, and I was a bit worried to see how thin and tired-looking she'd become over the past few weeks. She joked that it was fashionable, but I couldn't help noticing that she spent ages preparing delicious meals, but hardly ate anything. I started taking little treats round when I visited, in the hope of tempting her, and it became like an in-joke between us so that she would wiggle her eyebrows every time I handed over a paper bag with the latest delicacy in it.

Mum phoned twice a week and at Amy's mum's insistence, I spoke to her briefly each time. She apologised for the ghastly time I'd had at Ivy House, and said that she should have been firmer with the Community and protected me more. That thawed the ice between us a bit, though I couldn't help still feeling resentful. But it did start to seem that there might be some possibility of building a bridge over the huge abyss that yawned between us.

Chapter Thirty-eight

Birthday

The days ticked by to my fifteenth birthday – a Saturday, fortunately! Amy's parents offered to throw a party for me, and Estelle suggested that we go for lunch together, as Kieran was recording in London that day and wouldn't be home until the evening. He promised to be back in time for the party, saying he wouldn't miss it for the world.

'Of course, you may prefer to have lunch with your friends,' Estelle told me modestly, and I shook my head.

'I'd love to go out with you. Amy's meeting me in town at three o'clock, to go clothes shopping – will that give us enough time?' I asked. It was all arranged.

The day arrived. Fifteen – yay! I woke to find that Amy had crept out of bed to bring up cards and presents and a mug of my favourite hot chocolate with mint. We sat on the bed together, sipping our chocolate, and I opened the cards first. There was one from Mum and Dom, a funny cartoon one from Amy that we giggled over, several from my friends, and a heart-shaped card from Kieran which I kissed passionately. Nothing from Dad, which didn't surprise me. The love rat seemed to have vanished from our lives altogether.

My presents made me gasp with delight. I still hadn't really got used to having (and keeping) belongings after the sparseness of Ivy House. Amy gave me a beautiful black glittery top and a bright pink miniskirt, which I immediately vowed to wear for the party. Her parents gave me a set of the special hair straighteners that I loved so much. I shed a few tears over those presents. And Mum and Dom sent a necklace, earrings, and bracelet that they'd made for me from old cutlery. They were actually really pretty – the metal had a greenish tinge, and the jewellery was delicate, with little hearts and spirals all linked together. It looked good with my new clothes, and I promised to lend it to Amy after my birthday because she admired the set so much.

We had a special breakfast with Amy's parents, and lounged around listening to music and doing our make-up and hair all morning, then Amy went to meet Scotty and I skipped to Kieran's house to call for Estelle. Thomas and Estelle greeted me by singing *Happy Birthday* in harmony, which made me laugh, and gave me a perfume called Roseterie, which made me feel very grown up! It smelled of vanilla and roses and something spicy (Estelle thought it must be cinnamon), and I sprayed some on and Estelle sniffed it and said I smelled delicious. Arm in arm we strolled to the restaurant next to the Theatre Royal, where she had booked a table for two.

'Today we have two celebrations,' Estelle told me, her eyes twinkling.

'Two?'

'Yes! Your birthday, and we just heard that Thomas' new novel has just been shortlisted for a prize!'

I squealed with delight! Clearly Thomas' fountain was working its magic though, from what I'd heard, his books were very, very good even if he didn't have a fountain tinkling in his writing room. We raised our glasses to toast him, then raised them again to toast my birthday, then I declared a toast to Estelle as the Best mum in the World. She smiled, but looked as if she might cry.

'Are you OK?' I asked anxiously.

Estelle patted my arm. 'I'm better than OK, Lainey. I am a very lucky woman to have so much love in my life.'

We raised a toast to love.

Amy and I wandered around the shops afterwards (she loved my perfume, so I insisted that she wear some, too). When we arrived 'home' (as I now thought of Amy's house), Amy's mum was setting out plates of food, and Amy and her dad started to wind fairy lights around the top of the picture rails. I helped, and we giggled as we took it in turns to stand on the ladder and pretended to drape them around our hair before tacking them up properly. The room looked beautiful, like a grotto, and I kept saying over and over that I'd never, ever had such an amazing birthday. Amy's dad grinned at me.

'It's not over yet – there are more surprises to come,' he said, and then put his finger to his lips, signalling that he wasn't going to say another word. Amy and I did a gleeful little dance, whirling around the room until we fell in a giggling heap.

We showered and put on make-up again, and sprayed ourselves with my lush perfume, and wriggled into our party clothes. Amy wore a teal green dress with pointy handkerchief edges that made her look even more like a fairy. An hour before the party was due to start, just as we were going downstairs, the doorbell rang. My heart leaped in case it was Kieran, but when I answered the door I was utterly speechless. Standing on the doorstep, smiling broadly, were Mum and Dom.

Chapter Thirty-nine

More Surprises

Now I know that you probably think I'm cold-hearted and ungrateful. But I hadn't seen Mum for quite a while, and I really liked the jewellery she and Dom had sent. But when you are fifteen years (and a few hours) old, the last thing you expect (or want) is for your idiotsyncratic, estranged mum to turn up for your birthday party! To arrive that day is OK, I suppose, though I still hadn't forgiven her for putting me through Hell. But *purleeeease*, even parents you actually *like* are not the perfect party guests!

My shock and (well, yes, I have to admit) horror must have been evident, because Mum's smile faded a bit, though she stepped forward to give me a little hug, crying out, 'Surprise!' Dom, thank goodness, made no attempt to hug me.

'Can we come in?' Mum asked. I nodded, a trifle sullenly, and stepped back to let them pass. Amy's mum was just coming down the stairs, and she called out a greeting and said we should go and have a chat in the conservatory and she would bring some tea in. As she didn't look at all surprised, I gathered that this visit had been secretly pre-arranged. I peered out of the door to make sure no one else was lurking around, like the Dorm Demons perhaps, then closed it and followed Mum and Dom to the conservatory. We all sat down on the wicker furniture that tends to creak a bit.

'Happy birthday, Lainey,' Mum said, awkwardly.

'Thanks. And for the present,' I muttered.

There was a tense silence for a minute, then Amy's mum brought in a tray with cups of tea, and closed the door quietly behind her as she left. I stared at Mum, wondering what to say.

She smiled wryly.

'Lainey, I can understand you feeling angry with me. It hadn't occurred to me that you'd hate it so much at Ivy House, or that the other children would give you such a hard time.'

I shrugged. 'It's over now.'

Mum leaned forward. 'We have our house back. The tenants moved out yesterday, and Dom and I have just been there to leave a few things. You can come back home tomorrow.'

Suddenly I understood why Amy's dad's eyes had twinkled when he told me there were more surprises to come today.

'You've moved back to Bath? To our old house? With Dom?'

'Yes,' Mum said. 'And we have another resident there, but one that I think you'll be very pleased to see.'

I looked at her suspiciously. It flashed through my mind that they'd brought Aileen and Leila with them, which meant I wouldn't have a room and could carry on living at Amy's. I rather liked that idea.

'A furry resident,' Mum added. 'She's rather larger than when you last saw her.'

My heart almost stopped. I jumped up.

'One of the puppies?' I yelled.

Mum nodded, grinning. 'We bought Molly from the Community. She's yours now.'

Well, I have to say this for Mum. She is a Very Crafty Woman. She knew, just *knew*, that if Molly was living at our old house, I would want to live there. I'd missed her funny little smiley face and her soft, fluffy fur. My jaw was unbecomingly dropping towards my knees, so I snapped my mouth shut then leaped in the air, squealing. Amy popped her head round the door and smiled at Mum and Dom, and I dragged her into the conservatory.

'We have our house back! And we have Molly! Amy, I have a *dog*!'

It was pretty obvious from the ear to ear grin on Amy's face that she already knew, though it must have *killed* her to keep it secret from me. I wanted to rush round to see Molly, but Mum stood up, saying that my party was about to start, and they'd settle Molly in, and I should go home first thing in the morning.

Amy's parents came out to say goodbye as I saw Mum and Dom out. Her mum tapped me on the arm as we watched them walk away.

'Sometimes things turn out in rather unexpected ways, don't they, Lainey?' she said quietly.

I squeezed her hand. 'Yes,' I murmured. 'Sometimes they do.'

Chapter Forty

Party Time

By eight o'clock the party was in full swing, though there was
still no word from Kieran. The house was seething with people
and music, and the living room had been transformed into a
dance area. I tried to relax and enjoy it (and believe me, it really
was a fantastic party!) but had my ears tuned for the doorbell.
At nine o'clock I heard it ring, and ran to get to the door first.
Kieran stood there, his face one huge smile, and held out his
arms. I dived into them and snuggled up close, waves of
happiness washing over me.

'Happy birthday, Lainey,' he whispered.

I stood back, still holding his arms in case he vanished into
the darkness. 'You made it!' I crowed.

'Sorry it's so late, but the session went on all afternoon, then
I had to get the train home …'

I put my finger against his lips, feeling their cushiony
softness, and kissed him.

My present from Kieran was a tiny silver ring with a flower
formed from chips of ruby. It just fit on my pinky finger, and I
raised my hand to admire it, twisting it to watch it sparkle as it
caught the light. We stood just inside the door and cuddled for a
few minutes before going to join the others, who cheered at the
sight of Kieran and cooed over my ring. I did catch Dianne
shooting a Killer Glare my way, which made me feel a bit weird
for a moment, then she smiled and said how lucky I was, so I
thought perhaps I'd imagined it. After the trials and tribulations
of Ivy House it was easy to feel paranoid.

Whirling around the room with Kieran's arms around me,
laughter, music, and vivacious chatter filling the air, surrounded

by the happy faces of people who I had mostly known all my life, I felt as if something huge and joyous was welling up inside me and overflowing. I was home, with good friends, celebrating not just my birthday but my return to Bath. We had our house back, and Molly was mine, and I was in the arms of the BOMD. The nightmare was over and life was wonderful.

It's just as well that we never know quite what's around the corner. That night still shines as a pure memory of undiluted happiness. But a few days later everything was to change.

Chapter Forty-one

Back Home

It was strange leaving Amy's house, knowing that I wouldn't be living there any more. I thanked her parents for being so kind and for rescuing me from Ivy House, and silently determined to take round flowers for them later (and I did – I bought them a huge bunch of roses and gypsophila in the afternoon). They smiled and told me that I'd been an excellent house organiser, and they'd miss not having me around all the time. Amy and I walked down the road together, then separated when we got near the park. She was meeting Scotty and Rosa there, and I promised to come over in a while with Molly.

Our old house looked the same. I felt weird knocking on the door like a stranger or a guest, not someone who'd been born here (the tenants had been given both of our keys). Mum opened the door and drew me inside, smiling, and Molly came bounding up with an ecstatic welcome, hurling herself into the air and knocking me off balance, tail wagging in circles like a helicopter propeller. I put Horace's cage on the floor, dropped my bag and crouched down, and Molly leaped into my arms with such gusto that we both fell over. Dom came out from the kitchen and shyly said hello, and I realised that it probably felt a bit weird for him, too. I looked up and smiled at him as I rubbed Molly's tummy, and he looked pleased that the atmosphere wasn't hostile. Mum bent down and ruffled my hair – a gesture I usually hated, but I didn't mind. She looked happy to be home, too.

We took Horace up to my room, with Molly carefully negotiating the stairs, and Mum stood in the doorway while Molly hopped onto my bed as if she'd always lived here, settling down with her head on the pillow as if she thought she was a person. I unpacked my bag and put everything away. Even though there were far less possessions here now, none of the knick-knacks of my childhood or bits of paper posted everywhere with Mum's WOD (I'd seen no evidence of her Words at Ivy House, so maybe that was against the Rules there, too), the furniture was familiar, and my bedroom still held a slight echo of the scent of Black Orchid.

'How did you persuade them to let you bring Molly?' I asked.

Mum smiled. 'Oh, it didn't take much persuasion, really.' She rubbed her fingers together. 'Money, honey.'

I sniffed. 'So much for the right-on, self-sufficient, non-materialistic society.'

Mum sat on the bed next to Molly, as I carefully arranged my make-up and perfume on my dressing table, moving them a centimetre one way, then another, to get it all looking just right. 'I'm sorry, Lainey,' she said, and she really did look sorry. 'I was so desperate to get away from the worries here, and I thought it would be a good place for both of us.'

I perched beside her. The bed was now very, very crowded. 'Those people were really twisted,' I told her, quietly. 'But it's over now, and we're home, and I just want to get on with my life. Dom isn't going to try to turn our house into anything like the Community, is he? Because if he does, I'm out of here.'

'I think you'll find that Dom will fit in pretty well with our way of life. He was quite shocked at what happened there, especially when Sarah locked you up.' Mum stood up and stepped towards the door. I wondered whether to tell her about Creepy Lincoln and decided against it.

'What about money? And rabbits?' I asked. 'Can we afford to stay here? And are you still going to eat meat? Molly will *not* be trained to hunt.'

Mum gave me a long look. 'Don't worry. We're earning a good income with the jewellery now, and we both intend to get part-time jobs, as well. And Dom's quite keen on going vegetarian. It's chickpea curry for dinner.'

Once I started laughing I just couldn't stop. Mum joined in.

Tears were running down my face as I picked Molly up and we trooped downstairs together, still laughing. Dom, preparing vegetables in the kitchen, looked at us very oddly.

'Dom,' I told him, 'you are about to learn Mum's special relaxation technique.' Putting Molly on the floor, I leaned into the cupboard to get out a tin of chickpeas. 'If you haven't shelled chickpeas, you haven't lived.'

This time I did let him hug me, inwardly thanking my lucky stars that Mum had fallen for him rather than Creepy Lincoln.

Taking Molly to meet Amy and everyone in the park was such fun. Loads of people stopped to speak to me and pat her along the way, and she wriggled with delight at the sight of each new person. Amy was instantly besotted, and the others all made a huge fuss of her. Molly was in her element, graciously bestowing doggy smiles and licks to all. The horrors of Ivy House were receding faster with each passing moment, and life felt soooo good.

Chapter Forty-two

Papped

Amy came dashing up to me as I turned into the school gates. 'Lainey, I have to show you something!' she yelled, waving a copy of *Tween Dreaming* magazine under my nose. There, in the Breaking News section, was a photo of Kieran and me kissing at Amy's front door on the night of my birthday. I was stunned, and a bit freaked out.

'How did they get this?' I asked. 'No one was around!'

Amy shrugged. 'They follow people. Hide round corners and behind cars, and all that sort of stuff. Kieran's newsworthy lately. Now don't get upset, OK?'

Puzzled, I quickly read through the text below the photo. *Stunning Teen Star winner Kieran Kamau with Lainey Morgan, the girlfriend seemingly missing from the* Teen Star *finale, where he and his band Dark Matter won by the highest vote yet recorded. Kieran, tipped for a dazzling career in music and one of the hottest young men to emerge on the British music scene, left a recording session early to race to his girlfriend's birthday party. Watch out, Lainey. This guy is about to be swamped by offers, not all of them to do with music!*

'I don't *believe* this,' I croaked. 'They're being horrible about me! Why are they being so snide? I was locked up at Ivy House!'

'Paparazzi. They thrive on creating dissention,' Amy's voice was scornful. 'Just ignore it. I thought you should see it before anyone in school says anything, though.' She threw the magazine in the nearest bin, took my arm, and we walked up to the recreation ground with heads held high.

Everyone, but everyone, seemed to have either bought the wretched magazine or looked at it. All morning I was swamped by questions and plagued by comments. At lunchtime, out looking for Kieran, some boy I didn't even know pointed his mobile phone at me to take a photo and I snapped. 'Stop it!' I yelled. 'That rubbish wasn't even *true*!'

Someone touched my arm and I swung round. Kieran held his hands up. 'Whoah! Let's go to the field, away from the madness, OK?' I nodded gratefully, and we walked quickly, holding hands, to a quiet corner, ignoring the passers-by who called out to us. Kieran was as upset as I was about the magazine. He apologised, and I said that it wasn't him, it was *them* (whoever *they* were!), and we kissed and then sat close and picked at our lunch.

'I wasn't expecting this, Lainey. A bit naïve of me, I suppose, and Mum did try to warn me. I knew there'd be lots of press coverage, but hadn't thought about the gossip rats.'

I leaned against him and he put his arm around me. 'The joys of stardom, huh?' I muttered. 'Don't worry. They're just older versions of the Dorm Demons, and they'll move onto someone else soon. I hope,' I added under my breath.

Kieran looked into my eyes. 'I really do love you, Lainey,' he said. Before I could tell him I loved him, too, Dianne appeared, seemingly out of nowhere, and interrupted to ask Kieran when the album was coming out. I mean, how *inappropriate*, when we were clearly having a private conversation! The bell rang for afternoon lessons and the moment was lost. Kieran jumped up, pulling me after him, and together we walked back into school.

Chapter Forty-three

Fame

I read a survey a while ago. Apparently a high percentage of young people, when asked what they wanted to be in life, said, 'celebrity.' Not to do something amazing, like discover a cure for some killer disease, or discover an as-yet unknown species, or fly to the outer reaches of the solar system. Just fame for the sake of having their name known or their faces plastered on the cover of *Luscious* magazine – to be on *Big Brother* or some other reality show. Or to win *Teen Star*. Or to be linked with someone who's won *Teen Star*.

Well, Kieran and Dark Matter certainly achieved that generational dream. They were hardly ever out of the papers and magazines. Everywhere I looked, Kieran was smiling or smouldering at me. Billboards and buses advertising the forthcoming album, the pages of *Luscious* and *Tween Dreaming*, the internet, YouTube, MySpace, Facebook, Twitter. You name it, and Kieran's face was there. He was hardly ever around in the flesh though, and I missed him.

He was always rushing off for press conferences, recording, being photographed for something and, on his rare hours out of school or out of the limelight, he was trying to catch up with homework and cram facts for his GCSEs. When I did see him he was usually tired and stressed, which meant that he'd be argumentative – a side of him that I'd never come across before.

I took Molly round to his house a couple of times a week after school, in the hope of seeing him, but he was rarely there. So, instead, Estelle and I sat at the kitchen table and talked, mostly about him. I was worried about Estelle. She seemed paler and thinner every time I saw her but she laughed it off, saying it was old age creeping on. As Estelle was only a year or two older than Mum, that didn't make sense to me, but she gently told me off for fussing.

Kieran's fame affected me in other ways, too. The Paps, as Amy and I started calling them, followed me everywhere – but surreptitiously, so that mostly I didn't know they were around until someone pointed out photos of me in *Tween Dreaming*, looking thoughtful, or sad, and always on what seemed to be a spectacularly BHD. Captions like 'The Lonely Girlfriend Left Behind' were like knives driven into my heart, partly because it was all so humiliating, and partly because it seemed that they were very, very true.

And Kieran, when we did get time together, was changing beyond recognition. His gorgeous smile and spiralling curls were the same, but he seemed distant and (though I hate to admit this) arrogant. Kieran was starting to believe the hype about himself, and was full of how huge the new album was going to be, and how he was going to take up an offer to be in a movie. When I didn't see him I pined for him, but when we were together I felt as if I we were growing further and further apart, and it was hard to be the girl he'd fallen for. That girl seemed a stranger to me now, too.

I knew that the sudden fame must be hard for Kieran to deal with. With that, his music, the lack of privacy, exams looming, and the fact that he was still only sixteen, he was under huge pressure. I wanted to be supportive, but it was really, really hard to not get jealous or sulky when yet another beautiful girl threw herself at him, virtually (and sometimes literally) elbowing me out of the way. It seemed a long, long time since Kieran had said he loved me, and I had a sinking feeling that the distance widening between us was getting too vast to be breached.

So I stuck to my resolve to be there when he was free, which meant cancelling arrangements with Amy and other friends if he suddenly called to say he had an evening off. I felt bad about treating my friends casually – especially Amy, who had always, *always* been there for me, and who, with her parents, had rescued me from the jaws of hell. Amy, being kind, was great about it, but I still felt guilty every time I rang her to say that I was seeing Kieran instead of her. Dianne, Hannah, and Rosa didn't take it so well, though, and we saw less and less of each other as the weeks passed.

Then *Tween Dreaming* really, *really* excelled themselves. I never bought the rag (why should I fund their lies?), but there was always someone eager to show me the latest pic. This time it was Dianne who sidled up to me in the school café as I was queuing for some salad.

'Sorry to hear the news, Lainey,' she said sweetly.

I sighed, and shuffled into the gap left by the person in front of me. Whatever the news was, I didn't want to hear it. Dianne jostled me as I helped myself to salad. Some lettuce fell on the floor and I bent to retrieve it. An opened copy of *Tween Dreaming* dropped to the floor right in front of me. Much as I wanted to ignore it, I couldn't help seeing the huge colour photo of Kieran, arm in arm with Dahlia Dean, strolling along a London street. They both looked close and happy. I swallowed hard. 'The Perfect Couple – New Love For Kieran!' trumpeted the headline. Horrified, I dropped my plate and ran and ran until I was safe at home in my bedroom, not caring that I'd get detention for missing afternoon lessons.

Now, in case you've never heard of Dahlia Dean (and seriously, are you even *on* this planet if you haven't heard of her?), she's a sixteen-year-old supermodel, tipped to be the next Kate Moss. Dahlia is stunningly beautiful, with short black hair in a glossy bob, a perfect face *and* figure, and legs that go on for ever and ever. In that moment I hated her, really *hated* her. And I hated Dianne for gloating. It didn't occur to me until later that night, after I'd put on my oldest, raggiest T-shirt for comfort and wept enough tears to fill the River Avon, to hate Kieran. That lasted about five minutes before I started making excuses for him.

Chapter Forty-four

Excuses

- Kieran and Dahlia Dean were just friends, and *Tween Dreaming* was deliberately blowing it out of proportion.
- They just happened to bump into each other at the recording studio.
- They just happened to bump into each other at the TV studio.
- Kieran had a perfect right to have friends who were female.
- Just because he was seeing canoodling (sort of) with DD didn't mean they were An Item.
- They were walking arm in arm for a joint photo-shoot.

The Excuses kept me in one piece for about three minutes, then the insecurities kicked in.

- Kieran had dumped me without telling me.
- Kieran was in a relationship with DD without telling me.
- Kieran had never ever mentioned DD's name to me, so had been sneaking around behind my back.
- Kieran was a love rat of the highest order (or maybe that should be the lowest order).
- Kieran had no right to go out canoodling in public, knowing that he would be papped.
- Kieran didn't care about hurting me.
- My world had just come to an end.

Chapter Forty-five

The Morning After

The first thing I did in the morning was text Amy. *Hev u seen the pic?* She phoned me immediately. Dear, sweet Amy hadn't seen the photo. She'd been off with food poisoning (some dodgy fish), but had heard about it through the jungle drums set off by Dianne. As she was busy with her head down the toilet all day yesterday, she hadn't bothered to call Dianne back when she got her message of doom.

Trying (unsuccessfully) not to wail like something from a spoof horror movie, I blurted out, in between sobs, about the photo and the caption.

Amy, as usual, was a heroine. 'I'm off school again today because I puked half the night,' she croaked. 'Stay where you are and I'll ask Mum to drop me off on her way to work. You can't go out in this state.'

When I shuffled downstairs to fill the kettle, greeted with gusto by Molly (who always acts as if she's been parted from you forever, even if it's only a few minutes) Mum and Dom stared at me.

'Are you OK?' Mum asked.

I slammed the kettle down and switched it on. 'Fine,' I mumbled.

'You don't look fine,' Dom said, looking concerned.

I whirled around and gave them both a Killer Glare. With my red, piggy-swollen eyes and blotchy face, I was perfectly set up for Killer Glares that day. They both reeled back.

'Top marks for observation skills, Dom. No, I am *not* all right. The BOMD has been witnessed by about fifty million people in the arms of Dahlia Dean, and I am *most certainly* not fine.'

'There's no need to be rude to Dom,' Mum said gently. This was not the best way to comfort a grieving daughter, in my opinion, and my voice raised itself to a shrill shriek that scared even me.

'Dom is a *man*. Men are love rats. Why the *hell* should I be polite to him?'

Dom got up rather quickly and left the room. Mum stood up, looking angry. The doorbell rang, and I ran to let Amy in.

It wasn't Amy at the door. It was the Paps. The shots of me in just my raggy T-shirt, with a red face, swollen eyes, and tangled hair were all over the internet that day and in the papers by the following morning. *Tween Dreaming* had a field day and put their photo of me on the cover.

Chapter Forty-six

Kieran

Kieran phoned me the next day, wondering why I was plastered all over the media looking like a ragged, demented banshee. Mum answered the phone and I refused to speak to him. An hour later he was ringing the doorbell.

I was in my room with the light switched off, still in my raggy T-shirt, hair even more tangled because I couldn't be bothered to take a shower or brush my hair, or put on make-up which would only be smeared all over my face by tears anyway. Mum let him indoors and he stood outside my bedroom, pleading to be let in. After a few minutes I opened it and turned my back on him to go back inside. Kieran switched the light on. I quickly switched it off, but not quickly enough to miss his shocked expression, though of course he'd seen it all in the papers anyway. We stumbled separately to my bed in the dark and sat down. Kieran tried to take my hand. I snatched it away. We sat in silence for a couple of minutes.

Finally, 'That was really mean of the press,' he said quietly. I nodded, but of course it was dark so he couldn't see me. 'Why are you so upset?'

'Because you were out canoodling with Dahlia Dean,' I sniffled.

There was a long silence.

'Ah.' I felt rather than saw Kieran look away. 'It wasn't really anything ... she's just fun to be with.'

In that moment I knew, just *knew*, that he fancied her, whether or not they were actually in a relationship yet. And I knew that however hard I tried to be fun, and supportive, and not have BHDs, that Kieran was a star and had moved into a different world from me, and that it was over between us. And Kieran knew that I knew. He took my hand, and this time I let him, because it might be the last time ever that I would feel his hand in mine. His thumb stroked my forefinger.

'I'm sorry, Lainey.'

I started crying again. Great big embarrassing baby tears that made my nose run too. Kieran leaned over and kissed the top of my head, which made me feel even worse. There was no romance in it. 'You're a really special person ...' he murmured.

Just not special enough, I thought. 'Please go. Just go.'

Kieran went.

Chapter Forty-seven

Aftermath

Mum let me stay off school for the rest of the week, and Molly came to snuggle up and give doggy cuddles. Horace slept in my bed at night, curled against my feet (though Mum didn't know that – she would have gone nuts!). When I crept out of my room occasionally to get a drink, Mum spoke softly, as if I was an invalid, and she and Dom made nice, tempting meals that tasted like ashes.

I refused to speak to anyone on the phone. Most of the calls were fact-finding ones from Dianne and the crowd anyway, not sympathy calls. They scented blood and wanted to gloat. The only person I saw was Amy who, as usual, was absolutely amazing. She came and stayed for a few days, insisted that I switch the lamp on, even if I didn't want the overhead light, made me remove my raggy T-shirt for as long as it took to wash and dry it, talked me into lying in a bubble bath and washing my hair, and force-fed me special, hand-made French chocolates that her mum bought from our favourite chocolaterie.

On the third day I got dressed and put some make-up on. Mum had called in the Emergency Team (Aunt Bee and Uncle Denny) for moral support, and they cheered when Amy and I pattered down the stairs to join them at the dining table. Aunt Bee had a new film role, a decent one this time (as a hardy woman explorer – she said her lips would look chapped but her hair would mostly be dry, for a change) and she opened a bottle of champagne. We all had some, and then I ruined it by crying again because the last (and first) time I'd had champagne was when Kieran won the first heat of *Teen Star*. Aunt Bee leaned her elbows on the table and pointed her cigarette at me, emphasising each word.

'Lainey Morgan, you need to take some deep breaths and pull yourself together,' she announced in her most resounding thespian voice. I was so shocked that the tears stopped. Aunt Bee grinned. 'That's better. It's bloody awful having your heartbreak plastered all over the media, but don't you think it would do your self-esteem more good if you brazened it out?'

'But everyone's going to know Kieran dumped me for Dahlia Dean. And I can't bear the shame,' I whimpered.

Aunt Bee blew smoke over Mum (who winced and coughed – she doesn't like smoking either), and stubbed out her cigarette with a flourish. 'Whoever ended it isn't as important as the fact that you have a life to get on with. Put on an act, honey. *Pretend* to be brave, even if you don't feel it. Ignore the comments people make and they'll soon get bored. Brazen it out.'

I stared at her. She stared back. 'Sit up straight,' she said. 'Come on, stop slouching.' Amy and I both sat up very straight. I'd never heard Aunt Bee so assertive before. Maybe it was the 'strong woman' role she was getting into character for. I glanced at Mum. She looked quite stunned. I looked sideways at Amy. Her mouth was twitching at the corners.

'Would you like us to do a regimental march around the table?' I asked. Then I started to giggle hysterically and everyone else started laughing.

'That's the spirit,' grinned Aunt Bee, lighting another cigarette. 'Come on, girls, have some more champagne.'

It was very, very hard going back to school. Everyone stared at me and there were sudden weird silences followed by muttering and whispering as I passed the groups in the playground. In lessons the worst offender was Dianne. She made snide remarks about how the mighty are fallen and I realised that she'd been very, very jealous, but I took Aunt Bee's advice and ignored her, even though my face was scarlet. I avoided the areas where Kieran and I used to meet, and ate my packed lunch in the field with Amy.

To my surprise, although a lot of the girls were bitchy, most of the boys were friendlier than usual. Al Fredericks actually asked me out, looking very shy and pink in the face, and I was about to make a snotty remark when I stopped myself and said thanks, but I needed some time alone before getting involved with anyone else. Three more boys asked me out within two days. It took me a while to figure it out, but eventually it dawned that the boys seemed to think that some kind of veneer had rubbed off on me from Kieran's fame and my ghastly appearances in the papers. They thought they'd get their fifteen minutes of fame through me.

Chapter Forty-eight

One Month Later

I took Aunt Bee's advice and held my head high, even though my insides felt like jelly most of the time. I was papped for a couple more weeks before the press lost interest and moved on to torment their next victim. But photos of Kieran were everywhere I looked, and in quite a few of them Dahlia Dean was hanging on his arm and gazing up at him. The constant reminders made it very, very hard to try to move on. I resolved to focus on other things, and worked hard at school, did my homework (the teachers were absolutely and very vocally astonished, and I got lots of praise as well as good grades). I walked Molly every day, with Amy and sometimes Scotty. It was painful being with a couple now I wasn't part of one any more, but Scotty was so sweet and protective that I started to see why Amy liked him so much. He told me that Kieran had let fame go to his head, and that he was stupid for dumping me. That made me feel better for about three whole minutes.

Molly and I started going to puppy training classes once a week. It was fun being with other people who loved their pups as much as I loved Molly, and if anyone recognised me they didn't mention it. I was grateful for that. I made friends with Sonya, who had a hyperactive Cocker Spaniel, and we met up occasionally to walk the dogs together. Molly, the largest pup in class, could sit, give a paw, walk to heel, and lie down on command and I felt very proud of her.

On Saturdays Estelle and I had lunch together. She had phoned a few days after Kieran and I broke up, sounding terribly upset, and said that if I could bear to see her, she'd love for us to keep in touch. The first time, I visited her at their house when Kieran was out, but ended up crying all over Estelle because it opened up the emotional wounds to be there, so after that we met in town and tried out all the cafés that we hadn't been to. There are a lot of very, very nice cafés and restaurants in Bath, I discovered.

Estelle's health was seriously worrying me. She looked more gaunt every week, and I felt that if I hugged her too hard she would break. When I asked her for the millionth time whether she was OK she just gave a tired smile and told me she was fine – just a little anaemic.

Thomas had won the award he was nominated for! Estelle was so obviously thrilled for him and proud of him that I sent him a 'Congratulations' card, and had a sweet letter from him in exchange. Although we tried not to talk about Kieran, it was like trying to ignore an elephant in the room, so we did talk about him sometimes. He'd signed a movie contract and would be getting private tutoring for the time remaining before his GCSEs, because he was away so much. It was a relief to hear that I wouldn't be bumping into him at school. And his music was going well. From what Estelle said, I heard a subtext that she wasn't very happy about the huge changes that had come so suddenly. A couple of times she let it slip that he'd become a stranger, and then quickly covered it up by making excuses about how teenagers change a lot, even without sudden fame accelerating the process. But I enjoyed our weekly 'dates' as she called them, and it seemed that Estelle did too. We giggled a lot, and exchanged little confidences, and being around her always gave me a warm feeling.

At home, things were OK, though I felt kind of out of place there. Mum and Dom were very wrapped up in their relationship, and it was weird and very uncomfortable to walk in and find them snogging sometimes. Parents really should keep their loves lives private! Mum's WODs were back in evidence and we had chickpeas for dinner less often. I gathered that she was feeling less stressed. Their recycled cutlery business was bringing in enough money for them to work part-time and pay the bills, and there'd been no word from the love rat. Dom and I got on fine, at a distance. I think he was relieved that I didn't make a fuss over him being there, and he was actually more thoughtful than Mum a lot of the time, and did bother to ask how I was, and noticed when Molly had learned a new skill. Mum just seemed to float around in a haze of love, unaware that she had a daughter. Yuck!

Then something happened that made me realise how much I now looked on Estelle as my surrogate mum.

Chapter Forty-nine

Estelle

Estelle and I met outside Jamie's Italian for lunch. We'd just decided to order spinach and Taleggio croquettes, with me chattering away about how Molly could now catch a ball in her mouth, when Estelle suddenly went very white, slumped, and gave a little groan. I leaped up to put my arm around her and hold her up. 'Estelle, what's wrong?' I asked, starting to panic. She looked really, really ill.

'I'll be fine in a minute.' Her voice was strained, and I called for a glass of water for her. The waiter hovered, looking concerned.

'Shall I call Thomas?' I got out my mobile. Estelle nodded then, as I was searching for their number, she slowly and gracefully slid sideways and collapsed. I screamed and the waiter leaped forward.

'Phone an ambulance,' he shouted to the waiter at the cash desk, and diners turned around and craned their necks to see what was going on. I knew how Estelle would hate that, and I tried to shield her with my body while someone called an ambulance and I rang Thomas, who said that he'd be right there. I felt faint with fear and horror and gently, with the waiter's help, lay Estelle down on her side. Thomas arrived at the same time as the ambulance, and he put an arm around me while the paramedics lifted Estelle's silent form on the stretcher and took her down in the lift. I was sobbing hysterically by then, and Thomas looked sadly at me.

'I'll go to the hospital, and will come and see you afterwards. Are you OK to get home on your own?'

I nodded and followed him down, watching the ambulance

161

drive away with its sirens blaring.

Thomas rang the doorbell early in the evening, while Mum and Dom were still out goodness knows where. He looked ten years older and very, very tired, though he made a fuss of Molly when she wriggled ecstatically around his legs. I made him a cup of tea and we sat facing each other in the living room. I always associated Thomas with gentle calm, but he sat fidgeting, twisting his fingers together, then took a deep breath.

'Lainey, I have some very bad news,' he said quietly. I gulped and nodded, tears springing to my eyes already. Somehow I had known that it would be.

Estelle had ovarian cancer, which had spread so widely that by the time it was diagnosed nothing could be done except what Thomas called palliative care. He explained that this meant just giving her medicine to ease the pain. They had known for two months, but Estelle had insisted that Kieran and I were kept in the dark until it was absolutely necessary. Thomas had phoned Kieran in London after leaving the hospital and asked him to come home, saying only that Estelle was ill.

'Is she going to die?' I asked, my voice high with fear, hoping and praying that the answer would be 'No.'

Thomas nodded. His voice broke. 'Yes. Rather soon, I'm afraid.'

I moved to sit beside him on the sofa and took his hand. We cried together. I couldn't believe that vibrant Estelle would be taken from our lives, but the image of her, lying cold and pale on the stretcher, kept springing into my mind.

'Can I visit her?'

Thomas explained that Estelle would be at the hospital for a few days, but wanted to be at home as soon as possible. He said that it would be good for her to see me. 'She adores you, Lainey, and she was so upset about you and Kieran. But you must be brave. Promise me. It won't help her if you fall apart in front of her.'

I promised, and Thomas stood up. 'I need to go home and wait for Kieran to arrive. I'll pick you up to visit Estelle tomorrow afternoon, if you want to come.' Unable to speak, I just nodded, and walked with Thomas to the door. As I was about to open it he looked down at me with a tremulous smile. 'She loved you from the minute you met, you know. She always said you were like the daughter she never had.'

We clung to each other for a moment before he opened the door and walked down the path, his back bent like an old, old man. I watched his car drive away, then took Molly up to my room with me and curled up as tight as I could on my bed, struggling to grasp the magnitude of what Thomas had told me. There seemed no way to deal with the pain, so I held Molly and soaked her coat with tears.

Chapter Fifty

Looking At Loss

Thomas rang the doorbell at two o'clock, and I followed him to the car. It had only occurred to me that morning that Kieran would probably be there too, and I didn't have a clue as to how to keep myself in one piece. Fortunately the car was empty.

'Is Kieran with Estelle?' I asked tentatively.

Thomas shook his head. 'No. He took it very badly, and he's gone back to London.'

'*London*?' How could Kieran abandon his mother when she was so ill?

Thomas turned to face me as he put the key in the ignition. 'Lainey, there are several ways that people react to terminal illness. One of those is denial. Kieran can see that Estelle's very ill, but he refuses to believe it. And removing himself is his way of pretending that it's not happening.'

I was so shocked that I raised my voice. 'But how *could* he? What about *Estelle*?' I really, really hated him in that moment. Words like 'selfish', 'self-obsessed', 'spoilt brat' were racing around in my head, trying to get out. I pressed my lips together very tightly to stop them escaping.

Thomas started the engine. As we drove off he kept his eyes on the road. 'Estelle understands. It's a natural reaction.' We drove the rest of the way to the hospital in silence.

Estelle was sitting up in bed with a line snaking into her arm, wearing a pastel blue pashmina around her shoulders. Her face was carefully made up, and as I bent to kiss her cheek I caught a whiff of her familiar perfume. It made me want to cry, so I blinked hard and took a deep breath. Estelle smiled her beautiful, all-encompassing smile.

'Lainey, it's so lovely of you to come,' she said, with genuine pleasure and no trace of sadness or self-pity.

I didn't really know what to say, whether to mention her illness or ignore it. So I just said, 'It's always lovely to see you, Estelle,' and sat on the chair beside her, taking her hand. It felt papery and soft, and I could feel her slender bones under the skin. I sniffed.

'Don't worry, *ma cherie*. I'm not afraid, and I'm not in pain. Now, tell me all about what you and Molly have been up to.'

She was so natural, so much her easy-to-talk-to self, that I tried to ignore why she was here and told her all about puppy class, and how there was a Boxer pup called Squeaker who always did everything wrong. When his owner told him to sit, he lay down. When told to lie down, he sat. The command to 'walk to heel' got him racing off to play with the other dogs. Estelle giggled, so I thought of every silly incident from puppy class since Molly and I started going, and told her all of them. She loved it. After an hour Thomas stood up.

'Time to let you rest, my dear.' He perched on the edge of the bed and kissed her tenderly. Somehow it didn't seem yucky seeing Kieran's parents kiss. When he stood to leave, Estelle held out her arms to me and I burrowed into them.

'I'll see you tomorrow,' I whispered in her ear. She smiled.

'I'll look forward to it. Kiss Molly on the nose from me.'

'I will.' I kissed her soft cheek.

Leaving the ward, we both turned to look back. Estelle was watching us, smiling. We waved. She waved back and blew kisses. I smiled and blew kisses back while, inside, I felt that a huge part of me was dying right along with her.

Thomas wanted to speak to the doctor so gave me the keys and I found the car and sat inside, waiting. He gave me a wry smile when he slid into his seat. 'Estelle's coming home tomorrow,' he told me.

'That's good, isn't it?' I asked anxiously.

'She'll be happy about it,' was all Thomas said.

Chapter Fifty-one

Hello and Goodbye

Two days later I saw Kieran for the first time since we'd broken up. I was in Estelle's bedroom, holding her hand while she dozed, when he arrived back from London and bounded upstairs. His smile vanished when he saw me, then he pasted it back on, but it was a false one and I just stared at him. 'What are you doing here?' he asked rudely. I opened my mouth but no words would come out – which was fortunate, because just then Estelle opened her eyes. Her whole face lit up at the sight of him and she reached out her free hand to draw him towards her. I stood up.

'Don't leave, Lainey. But could you give Kieran and I a few minutes? I'd love a cup of tea if you wouldn't mind making one.'

I nodded and ran downstairs, away from Kieran's scowl. Thomas' study door was open so I popped my head round to ask him if he'd like some tea or coffee. Thomas was sitting at his beautiful desk, his head buried in his hands. I hesitated, not sure what to do; whether to tiptoe away or go in and put my hand on his shoulder.   I was just starting to quietly walk away when Thomas looked up.

'Umm. I was just wondering whether you'd like a drink. I'm making tea for Estelle,' I stammered, feeling embarrassed at intruding.

Thomas smiled wearily. 'I'd love some tea, thanks.' Then, as I turned to leave, 'You're a good-hearted girl, Lainey.'

'That's not what my mum says,' I joked, sniffing back tears. Thomas laughed and shook his head in disbelief as I deliberately winked at him. I'd been practicing my winking, because it made Estelle giggle.

167

I took as long as I could to make the tea, setting it all out with china cups and saucers, a sugar bowl and milk jug, and a small plate of Galette biscuits, Estelle's favourite, and took Thomas' into his study before carrying the tray upstairs. Kieran's eyes were red and I tried to avoid looking at him as I poured and distributed. I focused on Estelle, who looked exhausted.

'Estelle, I should go now,' I murmured, when she was comfortably sitting up with her drink beside her.

She smiled at me. 'Just stay a minute longer. Come, sit here, on the other side to Kieran.' I sat.

'I wanted to see both of you together. I know how hard it is for both of you – you were so close. But life moves on, old relationships change, new ones begin. Do something for me, please.'

We both stared at her. 'Look at each other. See all the good qualities that you saw when you first met. Even though you're not "together" now, you can still recognise what drew you together in the first place, and be friends.'

Reluctantly Kieran and I faced each other. I looked at him, setting aside my hurt and anger, and he looked at me. I saw his beauty, the extrovert wild streak that had so attracted me, his determination to steer his way through life and burn brightly. And I saw the pain and sadness and raw grief in his eyes, and wept inwardly for him. I was losing a dear friend, a mother figure. He was losing his mum. What Kieran saw when he looked at me, I'll never know. But he smiled, and reached across to take my hand and plant a small kiss on it.

'You're a special person, Lainey,' he said quietly.

'So are you, Kieran,' I whispered back.

Estelle laid both her hands over ours. 'You're both very, very special,' she said.

'But not half as wonderful as you are,' I whispered as I leaned over and kissed her, aware that Kieran needed this time with her. I said goodbye to both of them, promising to come over after school the next day. When I glanced back from the doorway Estelle was smiling beatifically.

Early the following morning Thomas phoned to tell me that Estelle had passed away peacefully in her sleep during the night.

Chapter Fifty-two

Friendship

Estelle's funeral was one of the media events of the year. Hundreds of people from the modelling and literary world came to say farewell, all dressed in bright, beautiful clothes, just as she had requested in the arrangements she had discussed with Thomas before she died. One thing that struck me forcibly was how many people loved her. It was, as Estelle had wished, a celebration of her life.

Photographers were everywhere, though most kept a respectful distance. *Tween Dream*, of course, did not. When pictures of Kieran, Thomas, and I standing close together were printed, I didn't care. Nor did I read the conjectures about Kieran and I just because at one point he reached for my hand, even though Dahlia Dean stood on the other side of him. We had all loved Estelle, and we were united in our grief.

Afterwards Kieran went wild for a while. I heard rumours about all-night parties and drunken behaviour, and understood that he had to let off steam somehow to stop himself from completely falling apart. It was over a month before I saw him again, and by then the gossip magazines were full of his split with Dahlia Dean, and photos of him with Jemmie, lead singer with The Chickadees. So I was astonished to answer the door during a makeover evening with Amy and find Kieran leaning against the frame.

We sat in my bedroom with Horace gently whispering in Kieran's ear, and drank cola that Amy had smuggled in (it was still banned from my house). It felt odd, and mundane bits of conversation kept starting and trailing off. After a while Amy put her make-up in her bag and hugged both of us. 'I'll see you tomorrow,' she told me. 'Take care of yourself, Kieran.'

He nodded solemnly. 'I will. You too.'

We both sat quietly for a few minutes after Amy left. Molly was scratching at the door, so I put Horace in his cage and let her in. She leaped onto the bed and stretched out, doing her groan of bliss. Kieran laughed.

'I can't believe how much she's grown! She's so much like Daisy now.'

We both gazed fondly at her. It was true. Molly's grey coat had thickened and lengthened, and she had a beard and long eyebrow tufts. Kieran took my hand and my heart gave a huge bump.

'I owe you an apology, Lainey,' he said. 'I didn't treat you very well, letting you find out about Dahlia through the papers.'

I shrugged. 'Up until that point you treated me very, very well. It's all in the past now, Kieran.'

He looked sad. 'I've missed you – not being able to talk to you about … things.'

I knew that he meant Estelle. She was in my thoughts all the time. 'You can talk to me anytime. About … anything.' I told him.

So he did. He told me about how much he missed Estelle, how nothing could ever be the same again, and how even achieving his ambitions seemed meaningless now. And Kieran talked about how hard it was to know who was a genuine friend, and who was only interested in him because he was famous. I listened, and held his hand, and we mourned what seemed to truly be the loss of childhood innocence and childish dreams. Then we talked about Estelle, and what an incredible woman and mother and friend she was, and I sobbed that I hadn't told her how much I loved her. Smiling wryly, Kieran said that I hadn't needed to. She knew.

'But do you know what I think?' Kieran murmured. I shook my head. 'I think Mum would want me to carry on – she'd want all of us to make the best of what we have, because that's how she lived. She was so pleased that I'd gone for the dream and achieved it. She was just worried that it might consume me and leave nothing of my real self.'

I smiled at him. 'But if you're aware of the pitfalls, you can avoid them.'

He nodded. 'We're doing a gig next week, in Bristol. Will you and Amy come? And Scotty, too.'

I touched his cheek. 'I'd love to.'

Chapter Fifty-three

A Fresh Start

Life went on. The Dark Matter gig was fantastic, and Amy, Scotty, and I cheered ourselves hoarse along with everyone else. I'd got into the habit of working harder at school, and my grades were very, very good. When Mum went to parents' evening she was speechless at the praise my teachers heaped on me. Kieran and I stayed in touch, talking on the phone every week and I visited him and Thomas when Kieran had free time. I missed Estelle terribly, but held on to the good memories because they were so precious to me.

Mum and Dom had hardly been around for weeks. They were either working in the studio they'd set up in the shed, or rushing off to their jobs, or wandering off, hand in hand, to goodness knows where. I felt like the adult, not the child, and became quite a good cook. On days when everything started to get on top of me, I shelled chickpeas.

So it was a big surprise to arrive home from school on a cold Thursday evening on the last day of Christmas term to find that Mum and Dom were actually at home. The fragrance of casserole drifted past as I opened the front door and I stood still for a moment, inhaling. Molly dashed up to greet me and I stooped to stroke her ears and ruffle the top of her soft, slender head. I threw my bag and coat over the banister and wandered into the kitchen. There, crowded together, clutching glasses of wine, was Mum, Dom, Aunt Bee and Uncle Denny, Aunt Carol and Uncle Todd.

'Is this a party?' I asked.

Aunt Bee laughed and took my arm to pull me into the throng. 'We just thought it would be nice to get together. We hardly see each other nowadays.'

It was a fun evening. Even Aunt Carol loosened up, and they teased Mum about finding Dom at Ivy House. I didn't think anyone had noticed my closed expression as the vile memories flooded back, and the conversation moved on to other things (like Aunt Bee's new role as a femme fatale, where she would actually look glamorous for a change).

By the time they all left it was late. Dom offered to wash up (at least he had proved himself to be domesticated) so Mum and I stayed where we were, in the living room. I stretched and started easing myself up to go to bed.

'Lainey,' Mum said in quite a nervous tone of voice. I paused halfway off the chair and looked at her. 'I'm sorry I put you through all that.'

'All what? It was a nice evening.' I sat down again. She clearly wanted to talk.

Mum coughed, something she always does when she feels uncomfortable. I sighed. All the signs pointed to an awkward conversation and I wondered what she was about to spring on me next. I hoped she wasn't planning on moving house again.

'Ivy House.'

'Oh.' There was a long silence. I moved to get up again and Mum coughed *again*. I sat back down, resigned to hearing her latest madcap plan.

She leaned forward, words tumbling out very fast, as if she was scared of losing them. 'I know I haven't been very considerate. I was so upset about your dad leaving, and all the money worries, that I wasn't thinking about how it was all affecting you.'

Well, what do you say when a parent goes on a confession spree? I just looked at her, astonished. There was a long silence.

'What I'm trying to say is … well … I've been thinking. I know this hasn't been an easy year for you, with Ivy House, and Kieran, and Estelle … but if you ever need to talk about anything, I'd like you to know that I'm here for you. And so is Dom.'

I got up and gave her a hug. 'Thanks, Mum,' I said. And went to bed.

Epilogue

It's peaceful by the duck pond, too early for mothers to bring their children to the park, though I can hear a few voices in the distance. I sit quietly on the bench, throwing chunks of bread to the ducks that greedily cluster around me, nudging each other out of the way. Molly lies beside me, panting after a long (and fortunately unsuccessful) pursuit of a squirrel, and I lean down to stroke her soft, whiskery head. She glances up, tongue lolling in her endearing smile. The sun is watery through a thin layer of clouds, and I watch a rat swim beneath the bridge and clamber up to the bank. He pauses and for a long moment we stare at each other, then he turns swiftly and vanishes into the reeds.

I think of Estelle and my heart contracts. But the pain and loss is less acute now, and I know that although she'll always hold a very special space in my heart, it will get easier to bear. At least Kieran and I are on good terms, which is what Estelle wanted. I think of Mum, and the slowly growing closeness between us. And I think of Amy and feel a wave of love sweep over me. I couldn't ask for a better friend.

Footsteps approach and pause nearby. A boy with a black Greyhound stands hesitantly on the path by the bridge. He looks vaguely familiar, one of Scotty's friends from another school. The boy nods a greeting and I nod in response. 'Do you mind if I sit here?' he asks, pointing to the other bench. I shake my head and Molly hauls herself to her feet and ambles over to say hello to both of them. I watch as the dogs sniff each other and decide to be friends. The boy rubs behind Molly's ears and, to my surprise, she flops down beside him, companionably leaning against the Greyhound instead of returning straight to me. The boy grins apologetically. 'Sam seems to attract other dogs. I think it's because he's so calm,' he says. I smile back. The boy strokes Molly. 'She's a Lurcher, isn't she? A Greyhound/Deerhound or Greyhound/Wolfhound mix, I'd guess.'

Surprised, I tell him that he's spot on. 'Her name's Molly,' I say. It always amuses me how Dog People exchange the names and heritage of their dogs (and sometimes have long conversations about their idiosyncrasies) but often forget to mention their own names. It's like a special club, really.

He looks nice. He's tall and slender, rather like his dog, with shortish, dark hair that flops over his forehead, and a shy smile which he keeps directing sideways at me. We sit in silence for a while, watching the ducks return to the water and paddle around. A seagull swoops low and Molly leaps nervously to her feet and returns to me. The boy and I laugh at the same time. I pick up Molly's lead and stand to leave just as he stands up, too. We both laugh again, sheepishly, and the dogs come to heel.

'I always walk Sam at this time of morning if you'd like to bring Molly over, too,' he says casually, as together we stroll up towards the top of the park.

Somehow I have a feeling that we'll be seeing a lot more of each other.

Romantic Fiction from

Accent Press

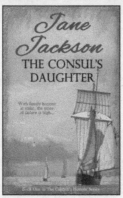

Nominated for the 2016 RONA Awards

Rosie Goes to War

ALISON KNIGHT

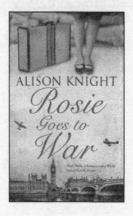

Stuck at her gran's house all summer with nothing to do, fifteen-year-old Rosie goes searching through some old junk and comes across a mysterious suitcase. It's full of vintage clothes, but when Rosie tries them on she finds herself suddenly flung back in time – into the same house in war-torn London.

With no idea of how she got there or how she can get back, she is soon caught up in a whirl of rationing, factory work, and dances. But Rosie comes crashing back to reality when she realises that if she can't find her way home, she may never be born at all …

THE DEEPEST CUT
natalie flynn

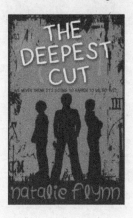

*'You haven't said a single word since you've been here. Is it on purpose?' I
tried to answer David but I couldn't ... my brain wanted to speak but my
throat wouldn't cooperate...*

Adam blames himself for his best friend's death. After attempting suicide,
he is put in the care of a local mental health facility. There, too
traumatized to speak, he begins to write notebooks detailing the events
leading up to Jake's murder, trying to understand who is really responsible
and cope with how needless it was, as a petty argument spiralled out of
control and peer pressure took hold.

Sad but unsentimental, this is a moving story of friendship and the
aftermath of its destruction.

For more information about **Lisa Tenzin-Dolma**

and other **Young Adult** titles

please visit

www.accentya.com